To
my beautiful wife

To Brett,
you are my inspiration ☺

XOXO

Yvonne

a.k.a. Nathan

Produced by:

FriesenPress

Suite 300 – 852 Fort Street
Victoria, BC, Canada V8W 1H8

www.friesenpress.com

Distributed to the trade by The Ingram Book Company

BOOK ONE
OF THE CREATORS' QUATRAIN

BLOOD
AND GODS

With the words we gave, the world was made
To write, we chose the everlasting
We opened death, to live forever
To die, we are reborn.

PROLOGUE

The wand refused to write. Once the ink had dried, using the sharp leather-bound eagle quill that constituted his wand did nothing but scratch the parchment, tearing into the dried, pounded-flat tail plants. And the source of his ink was in short supply, with what little remained in his small clay pot disappearing much too quickly. He had to work faster than he felt he could.

If he could learn the mastery of making vellum, he was convinced he could write books that would last long after his death. As it was, the parchment scrolls he used lasted maybe forty years before becoming fragile, dried out and brittle. If scrolls made from tail plant parchment were sealed in clay pots, they lasted a few hundred years at best.

The plants were stringy and weak, and when pounded flat were excellent pages upon which to write, in that they soaked up the ink readily and kept a distinct line between black ink and light brown parchment, leaving his words clear and easily read by the few who could still read. But the parchment's smooth scribability belied the underlying frailty of using plants that grew and died in quick succession. He needed to find a better way, and vellum could possibly offer it. But he was old, and besides his lack of knowledge, his weak hands could no longer manipulate the tools needed to

kill, skin, and prepare the animal hide for its transformation into a semi-permanent writing book.

His words meant more to him than his own life.

Perhaps his grandson could continue his work, Hrund thought. He'd taught the young man everything he knew, from his limited words to the art of finding and storing ink and making parchment. All of this had to be done in secret of course. If the father were to learn that both the grandson and grandfather were writing, they would be burned alive and torn to charred bits and fed to snakes. So engrossed in his work and frantic thoughts, grandfather never heard the footsteps. Perhaps he wouldn't have heard them anyway.

His last thought was one of shocked surprise at suddenly seeing his parchment soaked in blood. The blade had done its work so cleanly and effortlessly that the head, tumbling down from its neck and shoulders, still registered what the dying eyes took in even as it bounced off the table edge and thudded to the floor, the rest of the body soon following. With one swift motion the Sceyrah cleaned and stowed his blade back in its scabbard, concealed beneath the folds of his black robe. Sweeping all the parchments off the table, he strode to the crackling fire, and bending over the hearth, destroyed grandfather's dreams of a better world with one toss.

Before leaving, he made sure to mark the door lintel with his seal, the Krayven's head, so that all who entered and saw the horror within would know and accept why grandfather had died. The poisonous carrion bird that marked every Sceyrah, from the hilt of their blades to the tattoos on their face, the Krayven, provided all the warning anyone would need: herein lies a witch, a blaspheming demon, who has brought upon himself and all who love him this curse of death and destruction.

THE CREATED

The sun had just risen over Tratalja, and already it was quite warm. The light fog that had rolled off the river was now a faint mist as the sun burned it away. Winter was nearly over, and the hope of spring filled the air. Trees were budding, birds returning from southern migrations, and the City's market was thriving with more and more people making the trip each day to buy or sell much-needed goods. The cobble-stone streets shone with early morning dew like a patchwork of smooth time-worn river stones partially embedded in the muddy banks of the Eygil river. The streets closer to the gates were less fortunate, as their stones were usually covered in the mud brought in from carts and horses and people who rode or walked into Tratalja from the surrounding farm lands and dirt roads outside the City walls.

Every dirt road and tilled plot of land was experiencing the saturation that only spring can bring from all the rain and melting snows, so much so that it became precarious to load a cart too full of wares. A heavy-laden cart could easily sink into the muddy dirt roads and become solidly stuck. A few merchants had already

abandoned their carts and chosen to carry in their goods, the need to sell as much as they could more than motivation enough to turn even the skinniest farmer into a pack mule. The City was alive with noise and smell, the market teeming with life after a long hard winter. During the winter months the market's business slowed to a crawl, but now the shouts of vendors and the sounds of animals prepped for slaughter competed with each other in a never-ending cacophony: the sounds of spring within the City stood in stark contrast to the chirping of birds and the rushing of swollen streams that could be heard in the countryside.

The City was founded at the place where the Eygil emptied into the ocean, forming a natural harbor. The harbor was a wide bay, flanked by tall sheer cliffs of stone on either side. Many ships could lay anchor at any one time within the safe confines of these cliffs. There were always at least ten to fifteen ships tied to the docks, loading and unloading goods and passengers.

Thirty foot high walls ran from both cliffs, surrounding the City, with one main gate facing north and two smaller gates, one east-facing and the other south. The only other break in the walls came at the place where the river entered the City near the northeast corner. This vulnerable area required a higher level of security, hence the large contingent of guards on either side of the river that were permanently stationed to insure that no unauthorized boats entered the City.

The walls surrounding Tratalja were eight feet thick, allowing soldiers to walk along the top and stand guard at evenly spaced gaps in the parapet, the low wall that faced away from the City, protecting them from enemy fire. The City was large but densely populated by roughly eighty to one hundred thousand citizens, soldiers, and members of the Temple complex. Houses were packed close together, the City streets winding their way between domestic clusters like confused worms. Over the years houses had sprung up outside the City walls as well, as people longed to live as close as possible to the military protection and economic prosperity that Tratalja offered.

It was the day before Lilija's fourteenth birthday, or at least the day that the priests had set as her birthday. But it would be a day just like any other, she thought as she lifted herself out of her cot and surveyed her spartan cell. One small table held a bowl and jug that she used for washing up, and the only other piece of furniture was her simple straw mattress cot on which she could sit and sleep. There was a communal washroom down the hall, and she needed to use that before doing anything else. She quickly put on her cotton tunic and trousers and slipped into her only pair of shoes, a tight-fitting pair of leather slip-ons with a thin layer of fur inside. They were warm and comfortable from months of being molded to the exact shape of her feet. She was still growing, however, which accounted for the tightness. Soon she would be justified in asking for a new pair. She hurried out of her cell and down the cobblestone hallway to the washroom.

Some of her peers told her that she was pretty, with large brown eyes and the beginnings of a shapely body that boys seemed to admire. Mirrors, however, were scarce, so she rarely had the opportunity to scrutinize herself or work on making herself presentable. Not that physical appearance mattered all that much within the Temple complex. Her face remained unadorned, the tattoos that would mark her as a Sceyrah were something that waited until she turned eighteen. Her black hair was medium length, following the fashion of the City, and usually done in a ponytail to keep it out of the way when she was training or sparring. She was tall for her age, thin but muscular. It was cold in the washroom, so she hurried. When she finished, she was back in her room and just about to leave when there was an unexpected knocking at her door. She opened it, surprised to see one of the priests standing outside.

"Tomorrow is your birthday, as you know," the priest commented after she had let him in. "We have arranged a special match for you. You will spar with a boy two years older than you, whom you have fought once before. It seems that there is an increasing appetite amongst the citizens for fights, especially fights involving girls. There aren't too many of you, and fewer still with your level of abilities, so this fight should bring in a good amount of revenue." The priest began to fidget, perhaps feeling a little embarrassed at having volunteered so much information to a lowly trainee. He soon recovered, and began to look her up and down as though he were sizing up a piece of meat hanging in the market. Now it was Lilija's turn to squirm with embarrassment. "Be ready at dawn for the regular preparation rituals." Having said that, the priest spun on his heels and exited her cell, leaving Lilija alone with her thoughts.

She hadn't said a word the entire time the priest was with her, because she knew that to speak without being asked a direct question or being told to speak would result in punishment. But she marveled at the compliment: to hear a priest say that there were few among them with her level of skill was high praise indeed. The priests rarely spoke to the Sceyrah trainees, unless need compelled them. It would seem she was beginning to make her mark.

The precise day that Lilija was born was a mystery, since she had been dropped off at the Temple when she was a newborn infant. Lilija had asked the priests about her origins, but they were tight-lipped about any details regarding the children's lives before they were a part of the Temple community. The few details Lilija had been able to glean told her that her past was similar to almost every other child here: she was dropped off at the Temple by person or persons unknown. Had her mother dropped her off? A stranger, perhaps, who had heard a baby's pitiful cry from one of the City's garbage heaps? Her own name, Lilija, was unknown to her; only a few servants and a handful of priests within the Temple had

seen the inscription sewn onto the baby's swaddling clothes. And besides the priests, none of them could read.

The discovery of the inscription had led to a massive hunt by the Sceyrah, yet somehow Lilija's parents, or whoever had made the inscription, were never found. Numerous people were questioned, then beaten, but no one was willing or able to reveal the identities of the mystery parents. Finally the Sceyrah had given up, and the frustrated priests destroyed the cursed clothes, and after awhile everyone forgot about the strange circumstances surrounding this particular child.

Just this morning, Lilija had been present at the Temple gates when another child had been found abandoned outside. This was the way that parents usually got rid of an unwanted child, and in more desperate times, they resorted to even more desperate measures. Whenever the City experienced food shortages, the arrival of extra mouths to feed was not a happy time for many families. The birth of a child, usually reason to celebrate, often ended up with the newborn being suffocated and tossed onto a garbage heap. Sometimes the child wasn't even given the mercy of a quick death, and the newborn would be buried alive in refuse, thrown out with household scrap and what little food managed to rot before being eaten.

Now that spring had arrived, the main City dump would begin to smell stronger and stronger as the days grew hotter. On windy days, this posed less of a problem, since the prevailing winds came from the west and the dump was located directly downhill from the eastern gate of the City. But on calm days, the stench of rot would drift up and over the eastern wall, and those who lived on that particular side of Tratalja either grew accustomed to the odor or quickly moved on, finding a new home further west into the City or outside the City walls in one of the villages to the north or south.

Occasionally these discarded children were rescued by those in the City who happened upon their naked little bodies while they were still drawing breath and able to give a feeble cry, but only if the infant managed to wail loudly enough in one of the garbage heaps in the streets. Once those heaps were collected and tossed over the eastern wall, no one would hear their cries unless they happened to be outside the walls near the dump. Sometimes these rescuers would raise the child as their own, but more often than not they dropped them off at the Temple, knowing that the priests would be able to make use of the child. The laws of the City forbade infanticide, but such laws were ignored in tougher times.

Lilija was one of the fortunate ones, or so she thought now. For most of her childhood she had wished she'd been left to rot in the dump. Being raised in the Temple, being trained to become a Sceyrah - if she happened to be one of the fifty percent who survived past age twelve - was a brutal upbringing. The City had learned early in its history that if children could be taught to be killers, they made excellent soldiers, efficient assassins, deadly tools in the hands of their masters. As a young girl of fourteen, Lilija was one of only a handful of girls to survive to such an age within the Sceyrah. Her fellow trainees, for the most part, were boys and young men. All of them, girls and boys, were well on their way to completely forgetting any sense of who they were.

The Sceyrah was one, not many. They were the one, the elite. Lilija knew that if she reached the age of eighteen, she would finally be permitted to leave the Temple and enter into the service of the Sceyrah on the outside. She would be deployed wherever her masters felt her skill most needed. As a member of the cavalry, she could lead a troop of soldiers into battle. As a soldier within the City, she would be charged with upholding the peace of Tratalja and defending her against any foe, within and without. Or Lilija could find herself being used as an assassin, sent to the farthest reaches

of the City's purview. The primary role of the assassin was to exact justice on behalf of the lawmakers of the City, upholding its imperial rules for all those who pledged allegiance to the City's charter.

But for now she trained. Every day. And every day was exactly the same. Today, like every day, she had risen with the sun as the Temple bells had rung, announcing the start of a new day. The bells rang at sunrise and sunset, and also at the beginning of every main worship service in the Temple arena. The bells were located at the top of the Lord's Tower, in the center of the arena complex. Each tower also had massive oil lamps at their peaks, and these lamps were lit as soon as the sun went down, a tradition that had led to Tratalja's unofficial name as the City of Light. After the priest had left her cell she climbed the stone stairs to the main temple arena. The only thing different about today was that they were permitted to speak to each other. One day a week they were allowed to eat their meals in groups, and they were also allowed to speak to each other in between meals and training and exercise sessions. So when she spotted the boy she would spar with tomorrow at the top of the stairs she was climbing, she wasn't surprised when he spoke.

"I have been told that tomorrow we fight!" he said, the pitch of his voice suggesting that he was excited by the idea. "The last time you gave me a good challenge, although you fell pretty easily when I stopped taking it easy on you." This last phrase was delivered with an air of contempt, something she was used to from virtually every male, young or old, in the Temple.

"I have also been told about the match," she replied, "and I too remember the last time we fought. You indeed fought well against a girl two years your junior." The boy's eyes hardened, and Lilija was aware of the fact that since they had last sparred three years ago, he had gained a substantial amount of muscle weight. Perhaps she shouldn't provoke him too much, but the chance to speak her mind was rare, and she couldn't resist.

Lilija pushed past him in order to get to the arena, and he let her go, but not before whispering, "Tomorrow I'll break your other arm, Weyre witch." Lilija didn't respond and kept on walking towards the arena. Her nickname, newly acquired, was becoming a matter of pride with her. It was meant to be derogatory, but for her it was a sign that her strength was being noticed and appreciated. She reached the arena's edge and lifted the latch on the thick wooden door and pushed, and as it swung open she caught a glimpse of other trainees running on the track that encircled the massive arena floor. The quiet solitude of the corridor was replaced by the sounds of physical exertions: hand to hand sparring, weapons training, and a large number of out-of-breath boys and girls running the track that ran the entire perimeter of the arena floor, all serving to provide a jumble of noise. Shouts of triumph mingled with cries of pain. The seemingly constant pounding of feet on the hard clay track. The gasping, ragged breaths of the runners as they fought for air with every stride.

Here she too would run, barefoot except for the few bands of cloth she tied around her feet in such a way that they molded quite tightly to each foot's arches. Sometimes she ran until she nearly blacked out from lack of air, taking pleasure in seeing how far she could push her body.

Then she would eat, usually alone, although today she might take advantage of being permitted to speak to others and eat with a few of the other trainees whose company she enjoyed. The only other time they were allowed to speak, other than this one day a week, was when they were all together in the arena for hand to hand combat training. And then they were only permitted to speak to the trainee that they would be sparring with. They fought until one of them surrendered, was injured, or in rare cases killed.

These weekly spectacles usually drew a crowd, for which the priests sold tickets, so that the arena was nearly full with cheering

mobs. She had developed a following in the City. There were those who regularly came each week to watch her spar with whomever had been chosen as her partner for that day. As one of only a few girls, and as the one who was clearly superior, Lilija's fans grew in number each week. Lilija had even bested boys four years older than she, a true accomplishment. Although she was strong, she was clearly outmatched by most of the boys and young men in simple physical strength. This meant that she had to rely on skill, and so far her skill had proved to be a very effective counter to mere physical strength.

She enjoyed sparring. She loved the feeling of control over her body, of being able to execute quick, precise kicks and punches. She would flit about the arena, ducking, weaving, almost dancing to a silent symphony of martial song. No movement was wasted. Each step, twist, turn, and thrust of her body accomplished something. People began comparing her smooth, powerful movements to that of a cat, the Weyre. The "Weyre woman" was what they called her, named for the rare but deadly mountain lion of the northern reaches.

She had never seen such a beast. Indeed, few had, since they lived in the mountains of the north, rarely venturing down into the forested valleys directly south of their mountain range. And a good thing, too. They were massive cats, easily out-weighing a full grown man, and they were vicious. They could kill bears three times their size, and the few occasions that they came in contact with humans always resulted in brutal kills. They typically didn't eat humans, unless very hungry, but they always ripped them apart, leaving very little recognizable parts for those who discovered the carnage. It almost seemed as if the Weyre had a long-standing grudge against those who walked upright.

The crowds loved it whenever Lilija brought down a sparring partner that was bigger and stronger than she. Even some of her

fellow Sceyrah started calling her the "Weyre woman," although to give an individual in their midst a name other than Sceyrah guaranteed some sort of punishment for the offender. Behind her back, and only if they were certain they wouldn't get caught, they whispered the derogatory version of the name that the boy had used earlier, "Weyre witch."

She allowed herself a small smile as she reflected on being called a witch. It was meant to be an insult, but she took pride in being noticed. It meant they recognized her talent, at least. To warrant an insult meant that you had made an impression, and it had become her goal to impress.

She gently touched the scars that crisscrossed her wrists and arms. When she was younger, and every day involved vomiting up whatever little food she'd managed to eat in between training sessions, her only goal had been death. Five times the priests had caught her with a shard of pottery, a sharp stone, anything to try and cut open the veins in her wrist and arms, throat, or inner leg.

She had been desperate to escape the only life she'd known, but they had kept her under strict supervision for years. And now, approaching her fourteenth year, she had begun to take pleasure in her skill, and this pleasure fueled a desire for life. She still vomited sometimes, after a particularly grueling session, but she hardly even noticed. Pain and discomfort were of little consequence. She now bore the scars on her neck, wrists, arms, and inner legs with pride. They marked her own battle with herself. She desired, above all else, to mark others with the skill she had acquired. She had never killed a sparring partner. But each and every person she sparred with left with a mark, either from her blade, her foot, or her hand.

For the rest of the day, Lilija trained. After running in the arena, she ate, then trained with one of the masters in the art of

sword-fighting. His face seemed to brighten whenever Lilija joined him for training.

"The sword must not feel to you like a sword. It must feel like an extension of your arm. Every movement should feel as though you are moving your arm, and nothing more. You are using your arm to stab or slice or block your opponent." Lilija liked this Master. He never treated her like an inferior just because she was female. If he had a name, she didn't know it. Like all the other Masters, she simply referred to him as Master. He lived in one of the six towers that surrounded the Temple complex. The graduated Sceyrah had their own tower, and the Master Sceyrahs lived in this tower whenever they weren't deployed outside the City.

She practiced with the Master, dancing from side to side, evading his blows and responding with thrusts of her own. Long ago she had learned to ignore all other sounds. The sparring of other trainees, their shouts and cries, the thunderous bellows of other Master Trainers as they derided their pupils for every failing, every faltering step, every missed opportunity to take down their opponent. Despite all these potential distractions, the only thing Lilija saw and heard was the sound and sight of the Master directly in front of her. Her blade never found its mark as the Master always skillfully evaded her, and now and then he would slip past her defenses and get his blade within inches of her body, stopping at the last second. She envied his skill, and every time he scored a point in their swordplay she renewed her efforts, always striving to get better.

Now, with the day drawing to a close, Lilija left the arena, glancing back at the seventh tower that rose from the very center of the arena floor. This was the Lords' Tower. The High Priests, along with the War Generals and the King of the City, met regularly in this center tower to decide on the most crucial matters that affected the City and the lands it had conquered.

It seemed that the Temple complex had been purposefully constructed so as to draw as much attention to itself as possible. Throughout the City there were certain buildings that rose two, sometimes even three stories high, and they were owned by the wealthier citizens. Such buildings usually had beautiful balconies built on the second and third floors, which overlooked the crowded streets below. But the height of these homes and businesses were dwarfed by the tall majestic towers of the Temple.

The arena was the center, but not the focus. The focus was the Lords' Tower, rising from the center of the arena. The other six towers were not quite as tall, but they were impressive nonetheless as they circled the arena and displayed their lofty majesty. Nowhere else in the known world did towers exist such as these, taller than the hills outside the City, and even as tall as some of the crags or buttes in the desert, or so it was said by the few who had actually made the dangerous voyage out into the endless sands of the southern reaches.

As Lilija left the arena by the large wooden door and began descending the stairs that led to her cell, she remembered that first fight with the muscled boy. He had broken her arm, sending her to the base of another of the six towers that surrounded the Temple arena. In that tower lived the Medicians, men and women trained in the healing arts. After two months, her arm was as strong as it had ever been thanks to their unusual methods. But Lilija never forgot the pain, and the precise location of the break. She relished the thought of a chance to spar with this boy again. In three years he had grown much stronger, taller, and leaner. But so too had she. And she had practiced a particular feint, a move designed to draw her opponent to open up their left side just slightly, exposing their left arm.

The feint involved stepping to the right while beginning to throw a right jab, causing her opponent to put up their left arm in

an attempt to block the anticipated punch. But the punch never landed, because Lilija halted the forward motion of her arm at the same time as she swiveled her hips and brought her right leg up in a quick, hard side kick, aimed at the upper left arm of her sparring partner. It was her humerus bone that had been broken, and her goal was to snap that exact same bone in the boy's left arm. Her revenge would be calculated and extremely accurate, marked by the very precision and skill that was making her famous.

The next day, Lilija got up and began the preparation rituals. To prepare for a fight involved ceremonial cleaning, followed by prayers of supplication and thanksgiving to the gods and ancestors. When Lilija entered the small chapel that stood beside the arena's main doors, she discovered that she wasn't alone. Another girl, about her age, was already praying. When she heard Lilija enter she looked up, and motioned with her eyes that Lilija should join her. So Lilija walked over and knelt beside the girl, who had been praying in front of a statue of one of the Creators.

"You are fighting today, right?" the girl whispered.

"Yes, and we shouldn't be talking," Lilija responded. "Not today."

"I know, I know, but I'm worried. I overheard two priests yesterday, at lunch. They were talking about you, and I didn't like the way they were speaking. I think they mean to do you harm. Please be careful."

Lilija liked this girl. She was one of only a few other female trainees who had managed to survive the brutal training that they had all endured their whole lives.

"Don't worry about me. I'm ready for this fight, and if the priests want to do me harm, there is very little I can do about that." The other girl didn't seem to be reassured by Lilija's response, but she kept quiet. After Lilija mouthed a few prayers, she got up and left the girl without saying anything more.

It was time for her to report to the arena and get ready for the fight, which would take place before lunch. As she entered the arena, she was surprised to see that there were very few seats left. It seemed that this fight had generated a lot of interest, much more than usual. The priest this morning had been right. And that would mean a fair bit of money for the priests. The boy was already in the small fight circle located at the base of the center tower. The crowds were confined to one half of the arena bowl, which was designed as an amphitheater, so that every seat had a good view of the fight circle. The other side of the bowl-shaped arena was reserved for the weekly worship rites presided over by the priests.

Lilija entered the fight circle and took off her shoes. She then wrapped her fists with tightly woven cotton bands, which helped to minimize the scratches and bruises that one would inevitably get after pummeling an opponent's head and body. When the fight began, Lilija moved quickly, to no one's surprise. Her first jab was meant to confirm in the boy's mind that he was fighting the Weyre witch, a girl known for quick moves that ended fights almost before they began. He blocked her right hand and followed with a quick jab of his own. She blocked then feinted, beginning to throw a right jab; he moved too quickly, throwing his left arm up in a block, and with one powerful side kick she snapped his arm, in precisely the same place as her own injury four years previous. He screamed in pain and fell, clutching his left arm, which now dangled lifelessly in his right hand. The crowd cheered, many shouting "Weyre Witch! Weyre Witch!"

So the derogatory name had caught on beyond the temple complex, she thought ruefully. It was probably a good thing, if it meant her name would give her power over others. After all, it was the only name she had, besides Sceyrah, and it did feel kind of good to be recognized above all others. This kind of individual recognition did not go unnoticed: the priests were only too aware

of how popular Lilija had become with the crowds, and after the fight, which sent the boy to the Medicians with a broken left arm, Lilija lived, ate, and trained in a solitary six foot by six foot cell for an entire month. Her feces were collected once a week, and the tiny hole in the center of her cell drained most of her urine. Such a punishment would have tortured Lilija a few years ago, but by this time she had become hardened to isolation and loneliness, and the month was something she endured as well as anyone could.

All the Sceyrah-in-training were taught to read as well. Not to write, of course. The words they learned to read were written by temple Scribes, or occasionally by one of the priests, and would aid them once outside these walls in finding those who dared to write on their own. All the Scribes, as well as the few priests who could write, would never know a life outside these walls. They were prisoners of their own intellect, their own talent.

Their ability to write marked them as a part of the very select few who were sanctioned by the City's religion and military to do so. And the City made sure that anyone who could write was strictly controlled. Reading was one thing, and although it also brought a stigma to anyone who mastered it, writing and reading proved beyond a doubt that you were a person of great and dangerous power. The priests taught that words, once written down, had the power to become reality, so that writing was a form of magic. Very few people were afforded the right to possess that kind of power and live, at least in the City's charter.

For Lilija, the end result was all that mattered: being the best, the smartest, and the strongest that she could be. And sometimes even beating those older and smarter and stronger than she. The most important end for her was turning eighteen, so that she could discover a life outside these walls. This was her driving passion. She no longer yearned for death. Now she longed to bring death, if that meant her freedom. She would do as she was told. And she would continue to do so in her adult years, outside these walls. By being the best, the smartest, the deadliest Sceyrah, she would make her name known, so that everywhere she went she would be feared and respected; and in that, she would find freedom.

THE CREATORS

Kallos was confused. The others were talking about staying here, joining the place they'd made: merging with the things that now lived, moving about the sands and plains, living in the trees and seas. *What would happen to them?* Kallos wondered to himself. This had never been done before. Their Mother had certainly not instructed them in such a course of action, nor had the stories that were told ever contained such a plot in the narrative. They were Creators, not Creatures. They didn't stay with the things that they made. They certainly didn't become part of them.

Mother had always said that their purpose was to make life flourish, in as many ways as they could imagine, in as many places as they could visit. Never had she even hinted that they could stay in one place forever. But Karris and Eluthuria were quite excited by the prospect. They were speaking of a new thought, a desire to see what would happen if they merged with the world; what would happen to the animals and plants, fish and birds, if such creatures grew up in a world that had been seeded with the very lives of its Creators?

This question, however, was only one of two questions that remained unanswered for Kallos, unanswerable until after it was too late. It was this second question that seriously vexed him. What would happen to the Creators after they merged? Would they become extinct in time, in the same way that certain plants and animals ceased to exist in worlds that had lived for many millions of years? Or worse yet, would they immediately die, their life soaked up by every other life form, their entire identities wiped out of all memory?

Kallos didn't want to die. He loved to create, to find new worlds, and create some more. If Karris and Eluthuria wanted to die for some strange desire to experiment with their own lives and the powers they possessed, that was their choice. The problem was, Kallos didn't want to be separated from them. In particular, he didn't want to be separated from Eluthuria. His love for her had grown into something more, and he wanted to couple with her, so that they would live together forever as consorts. They could create together, and make names for one another, as had happened many times in many places, where they were called gods and goddesses, or aliens, or heroes, depending on the place and the words its inhabitants chose to use.

Kallos knew all the words, in all the languages, in every world he had ever visited. Language was part of the beauty that he and his kin helped create. So many words, in so many languages, and they all described in their own unique way the beauty and wonder and uniqueness of every living thing that came into being. And that was the beauty of it all: every single thing they created was alive. To speak of inanimate objects was to speak nonsense. A rock possessed life too, it simply showed it differently than an animal or human would. Life existed, down to the infinitesimal level of sub-atomic particles and waves, and lower than that even. Life showed itself in behavior, and in how the bits and pieces of matter

interacted with one another. Every created thing is in relationship to everything else. This was most true when Kallos looked at human beings.

Occasionally some of the peoples in these worlds possessed strange powers of their own, and were able to mimic some of the abilities that Kallos and his kin possessed. But never had any peoples even come close to the kind of creative powers that Kallos and his sisters and brothers shared. So if they gave themselves over to the world they had just made, if they merged with it, what then? Would plants grow up to be strong enough to strangle lions? Would people rise up and become gods themselves? The thought was scary, much too scary for Kallos. His fears rose up in his heart and began choking out the joy he felt whenever a new world blossomed before him. He didn't want to see his power dwindle, to be used up by lesser creatures, and he most certainly didn't want to die. He had never died before, he had always lived.

Kallos loved his power. He loved to create, to see things flourish right before his eyes merely because he had spoken them into being. He loved his uniqueness, the ways in which his creations were subtly different than everyone else's. Every Creator's creations were unique, of course. Every single Creator had their own unique stamp, so that any one of them could tell, simply by looking, who had created what. All their creations fit together, there was always harmony, but there was also those special tiny details that made the works of each Creator as unique as the Creators themselves.

They had reached this particular world, newly made but as yet uninhabited, after a long journey through many stars. Karris, Eluthuria, and Ugappe, Karris's consort, invited Kallos once again to consider a merge. Ugappe had come to agree with Karris and Eluthuria, believing as they did that such an act was not only in keeping with their mandate to make life flourish, it was a furthering of that mandate. They would be able to make life flourish in such

a way as had never been done before, and they disagreed categori-
cally with Kallos's fears.

"We shall not die, as the simple beasts and plants do. We
shall merely change." Ugappe spoke, as he always spoke, with
such simple strength, that Kallos almost believed him. But deep
down his doubts rekindled his fears, and those fears rose to the
surface like a wave cresting suddenly over unseen rocks, and he
resisted his friend's words. He responded by speaking to the one he
loved best.

"Eluthuria, will you still join Ugappe and Karris in this? Or will
you join me in a journey through more stars than we can count, to
reveal more worlds than the peoples have words?" Kallos heard,
for the first time, the weakness in his voice, a kind of pleading
that hinted at the desperation and fear he was feeling, and he
hated himself in that moment. Eluthuria looked at him with her
perfect eyes, clear blue, and for the first time Kallos saw a hint of
pity materialize in her gaze. But also love, for they had all loved
one another, and been together for as long as forever was, as was
intended since the first worlds had come into being.

"No, Kallos, my heart is knit here, in this time and place. I want
nothing more than to join with our friends and make something new.
Stay with us, couple with me here, that we may be joined together
with this world and with Karris and Ugappe." For a moment, Kallos'
desire for Eluthuria nearly made him accept. Nearly. But then the
fears rose even stronger, and his pride, stung by his own weakness,
fed off fear and fed the fear back into his own stubborn will. In that
moment his spirit departed from the three he loved more than anything or anyone; except, of course, for the love he had for himself.

THE CREATED

The gods were dead. At least that is what some of the villagers were saying, and Ari was beginning to believe it. The village was divided on the subject, and many a drunken argument involved whether or not the gods still existed, and if they did, whether or not they cared about the affairs of poor villagers living in the northern forests. For Ari, there was only one consideration that mattered: if the gods were still alive, how could they let his Grandfather die, the one person who cared about Ari? It wasn't fair, it wasn't right, and every time Ari thought about the gods a bitter taste rose up in his mouth. He hated them, alive or dead. They had done nothing to stop what had happened. They had allowed a hideous Sceyrah to chop off Grandfather's head and destroy his most precious belongings, his books and parchments. Well, almost all of them.

A part of Ari still couldn't believe that Grandfather was dead. There was not a happy memory in his entire life that didn't include the old man. Whenever he wasn't helping the tribal council make decisions that affected the northern clans they were a part of, Grandfather was helping Ari learn the art of hunting, trapping, and secretly, writing. They would collect the tail plants that grew on the burial mounds of their ancestors. As they worked, often at night and always hidden in the dark recesses of the barn that the villagers had helped them construct five years ago, Grandfather would teach him to write the ancient words of power. Ari would soak the fibrous grassy plant, then pound it flat, and then do the process over and over until they had sheets of parchment drying on homemade racks hidden behind a false wall in the barn. For ink they picked wild blackberries and blueberries, pressed the juices out of the berries, and mixed the juice with vinegar and salt. The vinegar and salt helped preserve the ink while enhancing the natural dark tones of the fruit juice. This mixture proved very useful; it hardly ever dried out, so long as one kept it sealed in a jar until you were ready to use it.

But these memories were all he had left. Now he stood beside Father, watching the flames lick up the sides of the funeral pyre, and soon the stench of burning flesh filled his nostrils. The night sky was dark, the cold light of the stars standing in stark contrast to the blackness all around them. Everything looked clearer in the cold. The stars seemed to shine with a fierceness they never showed in summer. The trees that surrounded the village showed their frost and snow-covered limbs with extra rawness, a display of cold cruelty. Near the pyre the heat was intense, but Ari's thin frame shook with cold despite the heat of the flames.

He had a gaunt face, making him look much older than his fourteen years. His blue eyes were almost always sad, bearing the haunted look of someone who has already endured a lifetime of pain. He glanced at the burning pyre, felt nauseated, then tried to turn away, but Father grabbed his shoulders and forced him to watch. He hated him for that. Truth be told, he had hated Father for a long time.

He remembered with sickening clarity the first time he had heard Father beat his Mother. After the war between the clans, Father became a drunk, always stinking of the honeyed mead and stronger ales that were brewed by the men in the village. Getting dead drunk led to violent brawls with any man who dared challenge him, and then one night, after a particularly horrible shouting match between Father and Mother, Ari heard Father punch her, hard, and she fell to the floor.

Ari couldn't see what was happening, since he had buried himself as deep under the covers of his bed as he could. Unfortunately, however, he could still hear. He heard the crack of Mother's skull as it bounced off the stone floor of the hearth in front of their fireplace, yet somehow she remained conscious. He never told anyone what happened, except Grandfather. And from that day forward Grandfather seemed to hate Ari's Father almost as much as Ari did.

That night, after Grandfather's burning, Ari's sleep was filled with terrors. Every time he closed his eyes, he could see the flames devouring the only person he'd ever loved, besides Mother. He would awake in a cold sweat, then fall back asleep, only to be confronted once again with the horrors he'd witnessed only hours ago. Finally, after what seemed like an eternity, he fell into a troubled sleep.

Suddenly he was dreaming again, or so it had seemed at first. He found himself outside, in the cold and snow, wearing only his bedclothes. He walked barefoot through the thick white covering, barely feeling it, even as his feet disappeared under the fluffy white blanket that covered the ground. It was lightly snowing outside, the flakes gently landing on his cheeks. He was walking into the forest, convinced that there was something he needed to see. As he left the clearing that contained his home, he followed the game trail that led into the blackness of the surrounding trees, unsure what was motivating him. What could be in the forest that he needed to discover?

He found the main trail that led away from their end of the village quite easily, since the moon was full and the sky was clear. The forest was dense, but wherever migratory animals had traveled, there were clear paths that had been formed over hundreds and perhaps thousands of years. The villagers used this particular trail to travel between their village and some of the other clan villages beyond the hills that marked the hunting territory of Ari's clan.

Everything seemed so real, but the fact that he wasn't even cold convinced Ari that this must be some sort of dream or vision. And when he saw the cloaked and hooded figure standing just ahead on the trail, Ari's blood ran cold. There was nothing about his appearance to suggest he was different, but he radiated a certain strangeness, a queer sort of power. At first, the sight of a stranger struck fear into Ari, especially being this far from the village, and at night. But that fear quickly turned to terror, as Ari became convinced that this strange power-filled man was a ghost.

He had heard the stories. Ghosts, or spirits of some kind, would occasionally be spotted in the woods surrounding the village. Usually they would appear after a battle, when many people had died a violent death. It was said that they were vengeful spirits, the dead come back to seek revenge on those who had killed them. Ari was sure that this was just such a spirit, because the terror he felt went beyond anything he'd experienced before, and he was well-versed in feeling fear.

His fears were heightened even more when the man began to move towards him. Ari was paralyzed, and instead of the usual cold sweats that accompanied his fear, he began to heat up. The sweat dripped off his forehead, his bedclothes were soaked within seconds. Wildly he looked around for something, anything, to help him. His feet remained firmly planted in the cold snow, refusing to

budge from their place on the trail. And then he caught a glimpse of the man's face, and his fear was replaced with wonder. It was Grandfather, and he was smiling that kind warm smile he reserved for Ari.

As quickly as the fear had settled on Ari, it lifted, and he knew that this was not an evil ghost, and this was no dream. This spirit loved him. His feet came unglued, and he rushed towards his Grandfather, only to see him fade out of sight.

"No, no, please come back!" Ari shouted.

"ARI!!" It was Father, plowing through the snowy trail. His Father's voice shook him, and Ari looked around, startled. As if remembering a dream, he realized where he was, and that Grandfather was gone.

"Ari, what in the Hells are you doing out here?!?" Father yelled, slapping him hard.

"I must have been sleep-walking again," Ari mumbled, his head bowed.

"I was awakened by one of the council members; they met without me and have decided that we are banished until the blasphemer's curse has been lifted. We must leave now." Father grabbed Ari's arm as he spoke and roughly shoved him back towards the village.

Ari felt numb. When he had realized who the ghost was, he had felt elated. Grandfather was back! But then he was gone, and reality had come crashing through the forest in the form of his Father. And now they were being forced to leave the village. Where would they go? Nothing seemed to make sense. They hurried back along the trail, and as they neared the village Ari began to feel the elements for the first time. His feet felt like blocks of ice, and the sweat-soaked bedclothes were freezing to his skin. As they came into the clearing that marked the beginning of their village, he could see by the moonlight that all the sod roofs in the village were covered in an

ever-thickening layer of snow. What had begun as a light snow-fall was turning into a winter storm, the flakes falling faster and thicker.

Ari ran into their stone house, quickly changing into dry clothes. He put on the simple undershirt and leggings that he always wore, followed by the leather skins and furs that would keep him warm. Father had made it perfectly clear that they weren't waiting until morning. They would leave just as soon as they could pack up everything that they would need. Father came into the house and began throwing things into his hunting pack. Ari grabbed his pack and ran back outside, towards the barn. He needed to take the few items of contraband that were carefully hidden behind the false wall towards the back of the barn. His writing quill, a few scrolls of parchment, and the only leather-bound book that Grandfather had scribed that hadn't been discovered and irreverently destroyed by the Sceyrah. There was also one small pot of ink, still sealed, so Ari took that as well.

Racing back into the house, Ari added some dried fruit and meat, as well as some nuts, to his already full pack. He would also need his bow, a few arrows, and his blade. These would come in handy for hunting, as well as protection. Father didn't even seem to notice that Ari had left the house, he was so intent on packing his own things.

"Do you have everything you need?" Father barked at Ari. A small "Yes" was Ari's quick reply.

"All right, let's go." With that, the two of them took one last look around, and then they left, walking back towards the trail that they had just used. Before they had left the house, Ari's father had given Ari a large sealed pot.

"This is what remains of your Grandfather. The village council believes that these ashes are cursed, so we are banished until we have found a way to lift the curse. They seem to think that if we take it far away, the village will be safe. Perhaps they simply want

26

to choose a new chief, and this is a convenient way to get rid of me." Father's voice was full of bitterness. Ari didn't care. All he knew was that he was leaving the only home he'd ever known.

His pack was already full, but Father refused to carry the ashes, so Ari managed to make room to fit the pot. It meant stuffing his only extra clothing in between his leather skins and his undershirt. As they entered the forest, Ari permitted himself one last look at the village. The wood and stone houses were obscured by the falling snow, and as Ari looked, he swore that he would never return.

4

They walked all night and into the next day. Around noon they stopped to eat, but Father wouldn't let Ari eat any more than some nuts and a few pieces of dried fruit.

"There won't be many animals out right now, so hunting isn't possible. We must ration our food, and once the storm lifts we should be able to kill something and supplement what we have in our packs." For the first time, Ari didn't hear bitterness in Father's voice, only a kind of weary resignation. The full gravity of their situation was clearly weighing on him.

After they'd eaten, they continued walking. Ari was curious to know if Father had a plan, if he knew where they were going, but Ari was reluctant to ask. Too often he didn't get the answer he sought, and instead would get a reprimand or a slap, so Ari usually kept his questions to himself. His curiosity rarely trumped his desire for self-preservation. On and on they walked, moving through the snow-filled valley and onto one of the small hills that marked the outer edge of their territory. Ari wasn't consciously keeping track of days, but he knew it had been three days since they had left the village. They stopped to rest for a few hours each night, and it was never long enough for Ari. He was exhausted, but Father seemed to be in a hurry.

"Can we sleep a little longer?" Ari had pleaded groggily when Father had awoken him on the fourth day just before dawn. The firm slap gave him his answer, so Ari shook himself awake as he quickly rolled up his bedroll and tied it to the bottom of his pack. The snow made for a soft bed, and he hardly needed the bedroll since his furs kept him warm, but he was still glad to have it. The fire that they had made when they'd stopped for the night was nothing but ashes, so they didn't bother covering it with snow.

The fourth day on the trail started just like the others, but by the time they stopped to eat around noon, Ari was nervous. He couldn't explain it, but it seemed as though they were being followed. He hadn't heard anything, and he definitely hadn't seen anything out of the ordinary, but still he couldn't shake the feeling that someone or something was out there. When they got up after eating, Ari made sure his blade was within his grasp by moving the scabbard underneath his furs until the handle of the blade jutted forward, poking out from his left side.

As they walked, Ari kept glancing around. He took in the snow-covered pine trees, looking like they'd been covered in a thick layer of goose down feathers. He noticed the unnaturally quiet surroundings, no birds chirping, no squirrels chattering, which even in winter was odd. After awhile Ari's Father noticed Ari's watchfulness, and he told Ari to stop being so fidgety. Ari tried to keep his eyes firmly planted on the trail ahead, but his nervousness turned to fear, and he couldn't help himself. Every once in a while he would sneak a glance to his left or his right. It felt like whatever was following them was within reach. Just before dusk, Ari's fears were confirmed.

They had been looking about for a good place to camp for the night when Ari felt a blast of air beside him. Father had been walking on Ari's left side, and when Ari felt the wind he'd looked to his left, but Father wasn't there anymore. In his place was a mass of white fur, and when it moved, Ari could see the blood-soaked figure of his Father in the snow. Ari screamed, tripped, and fell

hard, scrambling away from the beast as fast as he could. It was a Weyre, at least that's the only thing Ari could think of. It was a massive cat, nearly invisible against the white snow, except for the parts of its fur that was covered in Father's blood. The cat was furiously clawing and biting and tearing at what remained of Father's body, and at the gruesome sight Ari threw up, the fear and repulsion getting the best of him.

The cat's head whirled around, staring at Ari, its ears back, bloody fangs bared.

...rip you...

Ari's thoughts were swirling, but those two words stood out. And then he began to sweat. It felt just like the trail four days ago when he'd seen Grandfather's figure. But this was more intense. The sweat quickly drenched his entire body, and began pouring off his forehead, dripping into the snow. He couldn't think straight. Everything became bright, brighter almost than the sun, so much so that Ari began to squint.

...rip you...kill...

Again he heard it, or thought it, he wasn't sure. He was so confused, the thoughts racing through his brain. Once again he felt paralyzed, unable to move despite his overwhelming desire to run. As the cat stepped off the bloody corpse that used to be his Father, Ari remained frozen on his hands and knees. He kept his eyes on the cat, his body frozen in fear but his mind wanting to know when he could expect to feel its claws and fangs.

...kill you...

No, Ari thought, ***Don't kill me.***

The cat froze, a mere three feet away from Ari. Lifting his head, Ari could see its body, stiff, tense. He could almost sense the beast's confusion. Could it read his thoughts? And was he able to hear its thoughts? It was worth a try.

Please don't kill me, Ari thought again.

The cat seemed to be as shocked as Ari was. The two of them simply stared at each other, Ari kneeling with his head raised, the Weyre crouching. The fur on its back and tail was bushy, ears flattened back on its bloody head, and its wide fierce eyes stared unflinching into Ari's. The Weyre's confusion seemed apparent to Ari, as the cat was still frozen in position, one giant paw raised as if to tear into Ari, the claws fully extended and dripping with gore. Ari was feeling the same kind of power emanate from this beast as he'd felt from his Grandfather's ghost.

There was power here, on this trail, and it was coming from all directions, inside and out, heating him up to the point that his sweat was pouring off his face like rain off a roof. It seemed then that some control returned to his body, and Ari knew he was able to move. Facing what must be his own imminent death, Ari began to think of his Grandfather. Despite his own belief that to make any kind of movement would invite a swift and lethal attack, Ari wanted the comfort of being close to what remained of Grandfather. Ari swung his pack off his back, and reaching in, took out the clay pot. The cat had hissed and snarled as soon as Ari had begun moving. Even though Ari half expected to be dead before he had managed to get the clay pot out of his pack, he had moved quickly and with little shaking. The Weyre, however, still hadn't moved; it simply kept hissing and snarling and spitting towards Ari. As soon as the pot was out and in front of Ari, the cat fell silent. It slowly crept towards Ari, its head bent low, and it began to sniff at the pot of ashes.

...*dead...powerful*...

A desire began to fill Ari, and against every reasonable inclination of self-preservation, against every possible reason in the Hells or on earth, Ari reached out and stroked the cat's head, filling his hand with sticky warm blood, feeling the wet fur underneath. Its tongue flitted out, licking Ari's face. And he knew then that this

beast, this terror, somehow knew Grandfather already, and now it began to know Ari.

Sanngrier couldn't believe his good fortune. He had found the Raptor's body soon after it had fallen. It must have been soon, because no other animal had gnawed on it yet, not that there were too many other animals in the desert. But still, here was a Raptor, fallen, the rarest of birds, the most valuable carcass in the known world. Sanngrier had decided to go for a bit of a walk earlier that day, as he found that after too many days underground he got a bit restless. So he had left the caves and ventured outside, walking along one of the ridges that flanked the only path to the cave system's entrance.

Raptors were born in the sky, or at least that is what he was taught. They always flew, or glided, on the highest of all air currents. It was incredibly rare to even see one in flight, despite their size. They flew so high that only a mountain dweller, one of the Waodi of the northern ranges, or perhaps one of the few Sand Scribes that lived and worked on the massive buttes that shot up from the desert floor, ever caught a glimpse of its beautiful flight. Sanngrier was afraid of heights, so he had never been tempted to climb to the top of one of the scraggly buttes, the massive natural towers that shot skyward, some of them looking like jagged spears at their highest point. The mystery of the Raptors, how the birds lived, never touching earth until they died, was one that very few had even attempted to answer. What did they eat? How did they rest? How did they reproduce?

But now Sanngrier was running excitedly back to the caves, looking for someone to come help him carry the dead bird back to the safety of the massive labyrinth of underground rooms, a labyrinth accessible by only one entrance, and carefully guarded. The entrance was a small gap beside a huge boulder, located at the base of a tall scraggly peak. To get to this boulder required walking down a long-since dried up river bed, flanked by towering rock walls. It felt like walking into a trap, so even if a person found it, they would be unlikely to walk into this narrow canyon.

To get to this narrow rock canyon gulch, and the labyrinth entrance that it contained, required weeks of traveling south from Tratalja, the City of Light; and even if a person or large caravan of travelers made it this far, you had to know where the entrance was, or you could walk right up to it and not see it. The Sand Scribes always chose their entrances carefully. And they were guarded by some of the most vicious yet silent warriors in the region.

The Sand Warriors wouldn't help Sanngrier. They never left their posts unless relieved by another warrior, and Sanngrier wouldn't be able to see one of them unless he moved, so to ask them for help was virtually impossible unless he witnessed a changing of the guard; and even if he managed to spot one, and ask for help, they would never speak to him in response. Their vows were simple: silence and violence.

Sanngrier was looking for a fellow cave worker, a Builder skilled in stone and sand mortar work, charged with building and maintaining the myriad of underground rooms, colossal caverns, and secret water cisterns that kept all the sand peoples well watered. Such a fellow worker would be more than willing to help bring in such a find as a dead Raptor. Not only were the feathers more valuable than gold, the carcass could be eaten. Food was scarce, but also

strictly controlled, so that no one went hungry unless some unforeseen calamity struck their desert. Thankfully, that was rare. The desert didn't change, and rarely did anyone dare make the arduous journey to try and find the treasures within the caves. The few who did try, over the years, always died. Either the desert killed them, or the Sand Warriors did.

Sanngrier didn't find a cave worker. Instead, he almost ran headlong into Aiden, a Sand Scribe and a eunuch, and Aiden swore as he stumbled backwards into the cave that Sanngrier had just run into.

"Damn it, you shame-faced little grunt, can't you see what I'm carrying??" Sanngrier caught a glimpse of Aiden frantically juggling a long sealed clay pot meant to preserve scrolls, nearly dropping it against the polished stone floor.

"So sorry, so sorry, but please hurry with me, help," Sanngrier fought to get his breath so he could continue, "to get the bird, I found it."

"What bird? What the Hells are you talking about? Get another Builder, I'm far too busy trying to keep this pot from getting smashed by fawning boot-lickers like you."

"But please, please, it is a Raptor." The instant Sanngrier said that, Aiden's whole body changed. He froze, then leaped forward, grabbing Sanngrier by the scruff of the neck, saying in hushed but frantic tones, "Quickly, we will carry it back here, show me where it is. We cannot let anything happen to it." Now both Aiden and Sanngrier were running out of the cave and into the narrow passage that led to the opening to the river bed.

Stooping so as to avoid the large rock that shielded the opening from prying eyes, Aiden led the way, with Sanngrier close behind. They reached the bird, a mere two hundred yards from the mouth of the ancient river, and between the two of them they managed to carry it back to the caves. Once the other Scribes in this labyrinth

heard the news, the cave that housed the bird was crammed beyond capacity. Carefully, the Scribes closest to the carcass plucked every feather, then reverently handed the bird to the cooks, who just as reverently carried the bird to the lower kitchens. The best feathers would be turned into quills, to be used by the Scribes. Soon a select few would dine on one of the last remaining holy animals on earth. Many considered the Raptors to be descendants of the gods: the divine clothed in feather and claw, with a beak the size of a man's arm.

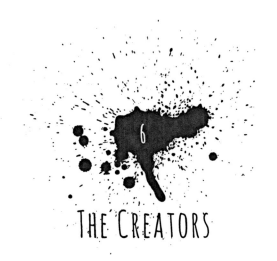

THE CREATORS

The sun and moon had come into being by the will of all four and the sun had finished its first pass and given its domain over to the moon. While this new world was experiencing its first night, Kallos made a plan of his own. The other three had left him, their spirits no longer united with his, and they had begun their preparations to never leave this place. They were sinking into a sleep from which they would never wake, and their bodies, their perfect celestial inspired bodies, would rot and decay and become earth. Kallos shuddered at the thought. That night, while their eternal sleep overtook their naked forms, Kallos found them on top of a mountain. The three looked so peaceful, he thought, as he knelt beside Eluthuria and gazed with longing at her perfect face, her blue eyes now hidden as they remained shut against the dark night sky.

It appeared that they had written words on their torsos before they'd succumbed to sleep, and they were words Kallos recognized but hadn't seen in these particular combinations. He grew bitter at the sight, reading the story that they had written without him, a story of new things being done, new ways of living with the works of their hands. Kallos felt anger rising, the heat of it in his chest and arms. They were going through with it, they were leaving him, especially Eluthuria, and he would no longer be a part of their stories. But Kallos was making up a story too, a plan that would allow him to get all he wanted without having to make the ultimate sacrifice.

Gathering his strength and courage, Kallos drew his finger slowly across Eluthuria's throat, opening it up as he did so. Her blood gushed out, instantly soaking her chest, pouring down into the rough rocks and dirt of this lonely mountain peak.

Her eyes flickered open briefly, confused and alarmed, but they shut almost as quickly as they'd opened. Collecting her blood in a rock he'd made just moments earlier, perfectly hollowed, a perfect sphere, a further mad desire stole over him, and he filled the palm of his right hand with the blood that still flowed from her neck, and he raised it to his lips and drank. Then his eyes were opened to something new, something dark and vile he'd never seen before, and without knowing how or why, he found himself changing, apart from any desire he possessed or any power of change his will could exert. Soon his form would be gone forever, a mere shadow the only thing that would remain of his body. He didn't know how he knew this, but he knew it, as certainly as he knew that it was all his doing.

With a growing terror and loathing, Kallos realized he had undone everything that he'd set out to do. He would remain immortal, yes, but now, because he'd killed and drank from the very source of life, he would become a shadow, imprisoned in this place.

He would never create again, not in this world or any other world, and he most certainly would never be able to use this stolen blood to create for himself the perfect partner, as he had planned to do. All this knowledge flooded his mind, overwhelmed his heart and soul, in the tiniest fraction of a second. He frantically looked at the words on the bodies of his partners, but they were meaningless to him now, strange swirls and patterns, markings that may as well have been the scratchings of a bear on an oak tree.

His powers were gone, and any thoughts he had of creating anything were instantly twisted into visions of darkness and evil that were as loathsome to him as his new form, the shadowy thing that could only be seen when all light was absent. Creation only happened through them, through him and his kin, and to create through something required that the thing through which the creation emerged was able to possess its own reality fully. A shadow was nothing, a non-reality, a barrenness that utterly lacked, in every way imaginable, that which was necessary to conduct all life. He now nearly completely lacked physical form, and as his last act before the shadow became everything, he sobbed and screamed and thrashed at his former love, shredding her body, until nothing was left but a fine red mist, a mist that was gently carried down the mountain in the soft night breeze.

THE CREATED

The Blood-eaters found Ari's body five days after the Weyre attack, half a day's walk from where the attack had happened. Ari had not left the spot where his Father's remains lay for four days, and for those four days the Weyre and Ari had camped, Ari not knowing what to do, and the Weyre seemingly content to stay with him. On the second day, Ari had awoken to find half a deer's carcass laying next to him, the other half being devoured by the massive cat. She never came too close to Ari, but she rarely ventured out of sight either. While Ari was trying to decide where to go from here, she seemed to be deciding what to do with Ari. Ari butchered some of the meat and enjoyed the first big meal he'd had since leaving his village.

On the fifth day since the attack, Ari decided it was time to leave. He still didn't know where to go, but it seemed that heading south made sense, so he packed his things and started walking. The Weyre padded silently behind Ari, and as they walked Ari would glance behind him now and then, just to make sure she was still there. Better to be able to see her, he thought, because that

meant she wasn't planning on killing him. They walked through the snowy forest, Ari forgetting the cold as his body heated up from exertion. It was tough going, walking through deep snow drifts, so that by lunchtime he was sweaty and tired. He knew better than to get too sweaty, since the sweat would freeze when he stopped walking and that could spell disaster. He stopped to eat some of the food in his pack.

He had just gotten the pack off his back when he heard the growl. He turned around in time to see the Weyre disappear into the forest, away from the trail. Was she hunting again? Surely she couldn't be hungry yet, after the deer from a few days ago. Ari began to worry. Had she sensed some other sort of danger?

The Weyre crept through the forest, keeping low to avoid most of the branches from the pine trees. She was silent, and in her silence she could hear the faint sounds of battle. It was a few miles away, but her hearing was acute. And her sense of smell was beginning to detect the coppery scent of blood. She began to run, dodging overhanging branches and leaping over fallen logs. Thin wisps of snow flew into the air from where her paws landed in the drifts, and after only half an hour she reached the edge of a clearing, within which stood a small village, or what was left of it. She had smelled the burning of the sod roofs, and now she could clearly see the after-effects of violent pillaging. She raced back towards Ari, knowing that the Blood-eaters who had sacked this village were heading directly towards him. She got to him first.

Ari had been walking for an hour or so after lunch when the Weyre returned. He didn't hear her until she was nearly on top of him, and then he screamed in terror as she pounced, her full weight crushing him to the ground, knocking the wind out of him. Before he had a chance to think, she was clawing at his back, ripping his fur and leathers to shreds, and then she bit the back of his neck. It felt like a branding iron, red-hot metal burning into his neck,

spreading quickly to his shoulders and arms. He tried to scream in pain, but all he got was a mouthful of snow. Suddenly he was flipped onto his back, and the Weyre began clawing his chest and arms, and then her teeth sank into his neck just under his chin. This time the pain was so severe that he passed out. It was here, on the path, lying in a mess of reddened snow, that the Blood-eaters found Ari's torn body, unconscious.

Brynhildur, the chief warrior of the Blood-eater clan, surveyed the area, alarmed. The tracks all around the body suggested a massive cat, a Weyre, and yet this boy wasn't dead. The Weyre never left a person alive. Brynhildur barked a few orders, and quickly two warriors lifted Ari's body and lashed it to one of their pack horses. They needed to keep moving, and Brynhildur wanted to find out what had happened to this boy. They continued on the trail, looking for a good spot to set up camp before darkness fell, all the while keeping a lookout for the Weyre in case she returned.

They found a good spot, a natural clearing, that would provide room for most if not all of their warriors and families. The Blood-eaters didn't always bring their families with them when they went raiding, but they had needed to find a new winter camp since the deer were no longer as plentiful farther north. Plunder accounted for much of their food and wealth, but they still needed to hunt for deer. Fortunately the villages in the southern forest hadn't been raided in years, so Brynhildur figured that they could amass a large amount of plunder whilst finding a more permanent place to call home during the long winter months.

They had killed almost everyone in the last village they had sacked, but they kept a few of the women for themselves, along with a few of the stronger men. Brynhildur's men needed wives, and they also needed a challenge. The captured men would provide that challenge. After breakfast the following morning, Brynhildur ordered his men to form a circle, so that they could test their strength against the village men. The captives were led into the circle, and Brynhildur produced a sword, gesturing to one of the villagers to take it.

"You will fight to the death. When you are dead, or have killed one of my men, your sword will be passed to another of your kinsmen, who will then fight."

The villagers were terrified. Everyone knew about the Blood-eaters and their love of fighting. It would be a miracle if one of these villagers managed to kill a Blood-eater warrior. But they had no choice. It was either fight, or die a slow torturous death at the hand of Brynhildur himself.

The first villager to fight was a large man, strong from years of farming and hunting. He gripped the sword so tightly that his knuckles went white. Despite the cold, his body was sweating profusely. The cold was no longer a factor. The fear of imminent death quickly countered the cold winter winds in the clearing, and the sweat-stained villager faced his challenger, a tall warrior, clothed in leather, with human bones woven into nearly every inch of his attire. His head was shaved bald, except for a strip of hair down the middle of his skull, spiked straight up with tiny bones woven into the hair near the scalp. His face was painted black, the whites of his eyes giving him an other-worldly look.

The villager shook as the warrior advanced. The fear seemed to propel the villager forward, and with little skill he frantically jabbed forward, trying to stab the warrior in the chest. His efforts were easily swept aside by the warrior's sword. The warrior could have finished him off then, but it seemed that he wanted more of a fight than what the villager was able to offer. The warrior backed off, then began to circle, the villager turning to follow his every movement. Once again the villager leaped forward, swinging his sword this time. At the last second the warrior ducked, and as he did so he slid his own sword up and to the right, slicing into the villager's arm. The man screamed and fell, clutching his bloody left arm, dropping his sword as he did so. Some of the warriors in the circle grunted, one of them grabbed the villager and heaved him back to his feet, another grabbing the sword and tossing it to the terrified man.

Once again the two combatants circled each other, looking for an opening. The warrior lunged forward, partially extending his sword, only to fall back with a smirk as the villager frantically tried to parry the thrust that was no longer there. It was like watching a cat play with a mouse.

By this time Ari was gaining consciousness. He couldn't figure out where he was: blood was pounding in his ears, his eyes felt heavy and bloated, and the pressure in his head was almost unbearable. After a while he realized he was hanging upside down from a tree branch, and there were warriors standing all around. He could feels the strands of what remained of his clothing dangling down from his upper body, brushing against him when the winds picked up. Whenever one of the warriors shifted the weight on his feet and moved slightly, Ari would catch a glimpse beyond them into a circle within a clearing, and he could see two men with swords. Would this be his fate too? Forced to fight to the death?

Ari had heard the stories. Blood-eaters only kept captives so that they could kill them in contests like this one, and then they would drink the blood of the dead. Ari trembled. And then he remembered the Weyre. He jerked involuntarily at the memory of being attacked, and he frantically twisted in the air, trying to see what his body looked like. The pain was coming back to him, the scratches and bites all over his body were burning like flaming embers from a fire.

Then he remembered the strangest thing. During a few brief moments of consciousness as he passed in and out of blackness, the Weyre had been licking the wounds she had made on his body;

47

although it may have been a dream, Ari could swear that as she did so, he could feel the wounds closing, the bleeding stop. He twisted and twisted, managing to catch a glimpse of his torso, scars now covering nearly every inch of his body that he could see. But no blood. His nearly naked body was clean, as far as he could tell. Maybe the Weyre had licked him, maybe it wasn't some bizarre dream. Why had she done it? Why had she attacked him, only to heal his wounds? And where was she now? He tried to find her with his mind, and he found that he could feel her presence, somehow, but he couldn't make out any thoughts.

When they had spent those few days together after Father's death, Ari had found that he could sometimes hear her thoughts, as he had when she had first attacked. And sometimes he could also feel what she felt. When she was eating the deer, Ari had felt a fierce sort of contentment. And when she had disappeared from the trail, he could feel her tenseness, and he could have sworn he smelt smoke and blood too, although he was alone on the trail, far from the ash of the campfire from the night before. It seemed that he and this beast had a connection, and now, as he hung from a tree, he felt even closer to her in his mind. Perhaps the bites and scratches forged a closer connection. He hoped that she would now come to his rescue and kill all these barbarians before they killed him. But he doubted that even a Weyre would be able to kill this many men at one time.

The fight in the circle ended. Ari heard the scream of pain, followed by hoots and cheers from those watching, and then he saw the dead villager being carried to a tree next to his, his feet wrapped in rope. The warriors lashed his legs to a tree branch, and as his body swung grotesquely, one of the warriors sliced the throat of the corpse, holding a bowl to catch the blood as it drained from the poor villager's body. Ari closed his eyes as the men took turns drinking from the bowl.

"Cut down the boy," Brynhildur commanded, wiping his blood-stained mouth with the back of his hand. Immediately one of the warriors strode over to where Ari hung, helpless. He managed to curl his head up to his chest as he fell, so that he landed on the back of his neck and shoulders, the rest of him crashing down, crushing him in place. Rough hands grabbed him by the arms and pulled him to his feet. He staggered, the blood rushing to his lower extremities, feeling like pins and needles were stabbing his feet from underneath.

"Who are you, and what happened to you?" Brynhildur was facing Ari as he questioned him.

"I - I am Ari, from a northern village. My Father and I were attacked by a Weyre."

"The Weyre do not leave boys or men all in one piece, let alone alive and sniveling. Why weren't you killed?"

"I do not know," Ari answered quietly, his head bowed. Strangely enough, his fear was subsiding, and now he felt a queer sort of calmness followed by a growing anger, a strength, creep into his mind and body.

"The Weyre must have had a reason. Perhaps you are a great warrior, and you fought off the attack." The men surrounding Ari laughed harshly, looking at his frail young body, their looks lingering on the fresh rough scars that covered nearly every inch of exposed skin.

"Perhaps," Ari replied.

"Yes, perhaps," Brynhildur smiled. "We shall see. You will fight next." Ari should have been terrified at the thought, but he wasn't. He simply staggered into the circle, the feeling slowly returning to his legs and feet.

"Give him the sword! And I shall give this little whelp the honor of fighting him myself!" Brynhildur shouted. The men cheered, several of them shoving Ari back and forth, leering at him.

49

Someone thrust a bloody sword into Ari's hands. He felt the hilt, the tightly bound leather straps wrapped around the metal handle of the sword. It was a simple weapon, and the last man to wield it was swinging upside down behind Ari, most of his blood now drained from his body. Brynhildur held a similar sword, but his was much more strange. Although it was similar in size and shape, it held an eerie quality. It was clearly old, for the metal blade was almost foggy in appearance. But what really made it different than anything Ari had ever seen was the writing, still clearly visible after what must have been hundreds, perhaps even thousands of years. The writing was etched into the blade itself, but Ari couldn't make out the words. They were unlike any that Grandfather had taught him. It felt strange, seeing written words on a blade. Ari had only ever seen words written in Grandfather's books, or on the parchment scrolls he practiced on.

Brynhildur followed Ari's eyes, and he smiled again.

"Do you like the sword? I will give you a much closer view." This pronouncement was followed by an eruption of more hoots and cheers from the warriors that surrounded Ari and the chief. Ari said nothing, and simply stared. His feeling of calm was quickly giving way to a rising anger. This was almost as unexpected as the lack of fear. Ari's anger began to boil into hate, and he imagined that this savage was not simply some pillager from the north, but rather was one of the Sceyrah, perhaps the very Sceyrah who had butchered his Grandfather. The more he imagined this, the more his boiling hate seemed to spill out of him in his sweat. Just like with Grandfather and the Weyre, the sweat was now pouring off him, the heat emanating from him as though he were a freshly stoked fire.

The chief saw the change in Ari's face, and his own face hardened. With a flick of his wrist and arm he brought his sword up, and he advanced towards Ari. Without thinking, Ari's sword rose up, and he countered the surging blade of the barbarian. Then, in a rush that felt like pure instinct, like an animal reacting to its foe, Ari raised his foot and kicked Brynhildur in the chest, sending him flying into the ring of on-lookers.

The cheers stopped. The warriors were shocked. Their chief weighed at least twice as much as this boy, and yet Ari had kicked him as though he were a small dog. Brynhildur picked himself up off the snow-covered ground and lunged again. This time Ari neatly side-stepped the attack and brought his own sword down on the back of Brynhildur's neck, severing his head from his neck. The spray of blood caught Ari in the face, and the rage he felt inside transformed into a scream of triumph. Holding his sword high, Ari screamed again, and the circle suddenly widened as the warriors fell back in shock and growing fear. It was becoming clear that this boy was no ordinary boy. He had just defeated their strongest warrior. And by the laws of the Blood-eaters, Ari was now their chief.

Ibn always enjoyed visiting the library in the High Priest's Tower, even if he could barely read. At least, that's what he wanted them to think. His reading comprehension was improving but he kept that a secret. It was permitted for the priestly class to learn some basic words, including the words necessary for simple commerce, as it was sometimes a requirement for the priests to be able to conduct business in the City. But to know too much was a liability: the more you knew, the more the High Priests and other members of the Lords' Council would seek to control you. Ibn had no desire to become one of the elite who were never permitted to leave the High Priest's tower. He got a thrill from reading, but his fear of becoming a life-long Scribe in the Tower trumped that thrill every time.

One of his favorite scrolls contained a re-telling of the acts of Creation, including some of the mythology surrounding the four Creators. They were the first to discover the power of the written word. In the scroll contained in the Tower, the story is told of how the Creators had created many things in the known world, but discovered that these things lacked permanence. It was only when they were written down, when the Creators crafted a written story explaining these physical things like plants and animals, that they began to have any permanence. This led the Creators to write the Book of Creation, or so it was said in this particular scroll at least. The Book of Creation was now a long-since lost scroll that describes in detail everything that the Creators wished to bring into being. It was believed that as long as this scroll existed, the earth and all it contained would continue to exist.

The idea of Creators, of gods, writing things down seemed strange to Ibn. Not for the first time, he found himself doubting the words he was reading. Surely the gods had no need to write in books like people did. Perhaps this scroll had been written, not as an accurate re-telling of the acts of the Creators, but rather as a cautionary tale, a tale designed to describe how it is that the written word is as powerful and dangerous as it so clearly was. The priests never seemed to miss an opportunity to remind the citizens of Tratalja about this particular story, and how it was madness for just anyone to try and emulate the gods by learning to write. If the very fabric of creation, if every plant and animal and person that existed owed its genesis to the written word, then to write was to risk a change at the very foundational level of all existence. This was the warning that the priests repeated at nearly every weekly worship service in the Temple arena.

Because of this discovery of the power of the written word, writing had been banned long ago. The priests not only feared what could happen to the foundation of existence, but also what could happen if someone wrote a story about themselves, putting them- selves in a place of wealth and power. Such a person could con- ceivably overthrow the entire city of Tratalja, and if left unchecked they could perhaps even undo the harmony of all creation and toss the world into chaos. Ibn, along with the other priests, knew that it wasn't simply the act of writing that possessed such unlimited power. The person doing the writing needed to have some natural abilities. Many village witches and sorcerers were born with certain powers, and these powers could conceivably aid a person in crafting a written work that would endure, that would alter the very nature of reality. The priests, however, hid this knowledge from the people.

According to what they taught the people, anyone who dared to write was running the risk of changing reality. This gave the priests an almost unlimited power of suppression. No one questioned the executions of writers, the use of the Sceyrah to hunt down and kill anyone who dared to put quill to parchment or vellum.

It was a mystery how the Sceyrah were able to discover the identities of those who wrote in secret. It was a carefully guarded process, and it almost definitely involved some sort of magic, but even for priests like Ibn the process was never disclosed. All anyone knew was that once in a while a Sceyrah was dispatched from the City, sent on horseback to find and kill someone who had dared to defy the most important of all laws that Tratalja sought to enforce.

Despite his attraction to the arts of the Scribes, Ibn enjoyed being a High Priest. It was only a select number of priests who ever made it to such a high position, and he had worked hard to get here. One day it would be his lot to visit the Oracle. Such a privilege was also a great thrill, and he didn't want to do anything that would jeopardize his role in the clerical order. So he remained content with his occasional visits to the library, usually under the pretense that he needed to read up on City business dealings. There were times when that was actually close to the truth. He was always thinking of ways to make more money for the Temple. After all, it wasn't cheap being a priest. The cost of training the Sceyrah, of conducting weekly worship services, and of presiding over every major spiritual festival in the City's annual life cycle was a massive undertaking.

Today, Ibn was reading a scroll that had recently been given to the City by the Sand Scribes. They rarely visited the City, but whenever they did they brought a gift, usually a scroll or book, and presented it to the High Priests. It was a tenuous relationship, the one between the Sand Scribes and the High Priests of Tratalja. The

High Priests were suspicious of the Scribes, always fearing their abilities and knowledge. The Scribes dedicated their entire lives to the written word, and had done so for thousands of years. The Scribes that lived in the High Priest's tower were like uneducated children in comparison. The Sand Scribes had always been able to remain an arm's length away from Tratalja's reach, despite a few attempts in the past by the City to conquer them and control their writing activities.

Ibn was reading the history of the Sand Scribes, beautifully detailed in the scroll laid out in front of him. *What a resourceful group,* he was thinking to himself, *to have created such an amazing labyrinth of caves.* Numerous labyrinths, actually, each one composed of countless underground tunnels, caves, and massive rooms, carved out of solid rock. One day he would love to visit, if it was permitted. Few had been given such a privilege, and he hoped that one day that privilege would be his.

As he was reading about the creation of a particular underground labyrinth some eight hundred years ago, he was interrupted by a page who came running into the library.

"Master Ibn," the page called out as he neared Ibn's desk, "Agathos has called a meeting of the Lords' Council, to begin immediately."

Ibn looked up from the scroll, surprised. "Immediately? Are you sure? This is the first I have heard of it."

"Yes, immediately, and Agathos told me to tell you to hurry." This was unusual. Meetings were held once a month, and in all his time as a High Priest Ibn could not remember when a meeting had been called outside of those scheduled monthly gatherings.

Ibn felt nervous as he rushed out of the library and raced down the stone steps, stopping only to acknowledge with a slight bow the priest making his way up the stairs as Ibn descended. Resuming his frantic pace, Ibn reached the bottom of the stairs and ran outside,

crossing the arena floor that was used solely for the weekly worship services. There were stone statues of the four Creators, as well as statues of some of the ancient heroes that the great City of Tratalja credited with its creation and protection. They were the ancestors that Ibn prayed to, and now he slowed down to a fast walk, not wanting to offend these powerful ancestors by rushing past them. He glanced up at the stone faces of the statues, mouthed a few brief words, asking for their wisdom as he met with the other members of the council.

The Lords' Council always met in the seventh tower, aptly named the Lords' Tower, which rose from the center of the massive bowl-shaped arena. Ibn entered the tower, pushing open the massive gold-encrusted wooden door, and started up the steps. He was sufficiently out of breath to negate the possibility of any more running, so he walked up the steps, wondering what this meeting could be about. He reached the top of the tower, and the large meeting room that was situated directly ahead as one reached the top of the spiral stone staircase. Another door, this one even more beautiful in its gold-leafed carvings, opened for him just as Ibn was about to reach forward and push. Agathos was on the other side.

"I was beginning to wonder if you had failed to hear of our meeting," Agathos smiled as he spoke, but his eyes remained hard.

"I was sequestered in the library, trying to locate a certain business scroll," Ibn lied, head down. Although both he and Agathos were High Priests, Agathos was the elder, and therefore the more important and powerful of the two.

"So we are all here then?" boomed a voice that could only be King Fadel. Not known for his patience, the King's voice was unmistakeable. A large but not fat man, Fadel was powerful in more ways than one. Ibn feared him. Even proud Agathos was slightly awed by the King. The Lords' Council was not a large group, and today it seemed even smaller than usual. There were not the normal

number of High Priests in attendance, perhaps owing to the unexpected and hastily called meeting. Besides Agathos and Ibn, there were four War Generals and the King.

"Please sit, Ibn," the King intoned. "I have called this meeting because my Generals have informed me of a very serious threat against Tratalja. The Blood-eaters of the north are on the move. Our scouts have sighted them as far south as the great bend in the river Eygil, where it turns south and leaves the forest."

Ibn gasped. The Blood-eaters never ventured so far south. The forest ended at the bend in the river, where the Eygil turned southward towards the City, and the Blood-eaters never left the forest.

"What can this mean, your Eminence?" asked Ibn. "In all of our recorded history, the Blood-eaters have never threatened any village south of the river's turn. Do you suspect that they will venture further south?"

"Our scouts have reported that the Blood-eaters are larger in number than ever," the King replied, "and they show signs of being prepared for large-scale war. We know that the forest peoples have had year after year of meager harvests and poor hunting, so perhaps the Blood-eaters have not been able to collect as much plunder from their raids as before. I have ordered six of our warships to sail up the western coast and see if they can engage the Blood-eaters before they have time to march south. The warships will sail up the coast and drop anchor at Land's Bend and attempt to catch the Blood-eaters unawares. This, however, is only one part of my plan: I also need to send the army. Unfortunately, we are lacking half our Generals, as half the army is still fighting in the eastern lands. I need the Sceyrah to help lead the army."

Ibn was beginning to understand. The King needed the Sceyrah, and only the Lords' Council could authorize their use. This would require the High Priests to give their vote of approval for such a plan.

"Your Majesty, the Sceyrah are limited in number, as you know, and half of them are with your armies in the east. We cannot spare the other half. To do so would leave the City vulnerable," Agathos spoke quietly, keeping his voice even.

"If the Blood-eaters make it past the warships, there may not be much of a City left!" the King shouted, pounding the table with his fist.

"We can spare a few, but only a few," Agathos continued, his eyes downcast, his voice small.

"A few??" The King's replies were growing in both volume and incredulity, and Agathos was the main target, causing the eldest High Priest to begin to sweat, a rare sight indeed since Agathos prided himself on his steely composure. Ibn had already slunk down as low as he could in his seat, and now the King paused long enough to look each and every person in the eye, ending with Agathos. Despite his fear, Ibn didn't dare avoid his gaze, because to avert one's gaze when the King was speaking was a sign of great disrespect, and so long as the King commanded everyone's attention, everyone's attention was riveted on the King. By now the tension in the room was palpable, like a fast-brewing thunderstorm, and as the King continued to hold Agathos in his withering glare he gritted his teeth and asked the sweating priest another question.

"I need more than a few." The words came out of the King's mouth with an obvious amount of self-control that kept them from being shouted. Instead the King's voice was quiet, almost a hiss.

"How many, exactly, are you willing to part with?"

"At most, fifty," Agathos replied, his voice even quieter, not due to self-control but rather the combined effects of fear and trembling.

"Fifty?!?" the King shouted. "I need at least one hundred, maybe even two hundred!" At this, Agathos sighed, but Ibn was thinking fast, and he had come up with an idea.

"P-pardon your Majesty," Ibn hated hearing the squeaky stutter of his voice when he was afraid, but he forged ahead anyway. "I may have an idea."

"Apologies, your Majesty, Ibn means well but he is still young." Agathos glared at Ibn, clearly annoyed that the younger High Priest had dared to interject.

"He may be young," the King replied, "but I need the Sceyrah to lead my armies. If Ibn has an idea of how to make that happen I'd like to hear it." Buoyed by the King's response, Ibn spoke again.

"We can spare fifty of the graduated Sceyrah, as Agathos has said," Ibn hesitated before continuing, "but we could also spare some of the trainees."

"Trainees?? They are not ready to *lead*! We need leaders, not children, Ibn!" Agathos, as usual, was dismissive, and his tone carried its usual condescension and scorn for Ibn.

The King's eyes never strayed from Ibn as he thought about the possibility of using trainees. The idea had merit, he admitted to himself, and a part of him wanted to act on the suggestion just to anger the haughty Agathos.

"Trainees, you say? How many do you have that have reached the age of fourteen?" the King asked. Ibn proceeded carefully, replying after a brief moment of thought. "To my knowledge, there are over two hundred who have reached that age, your Majesty." The King pondered this for a moment. He wouldn't need all of them, but if he could have most of them than he felt reasonably confident that his army would be well led.

"Give me one hundred and fifty, and I believe we can amass a force strong enough to defeat this northern horde of savages. Do I have your approval?" the King looked from Agathos to Ibn, and back again. Agathos fidgeted in his seat, clearly angry at Ibn, but also weighing the cost in his head. To lose trainees was not as bad as losing graduated Sceyrah. If they sent trainees into the

battlefield, that meant they could keep the majority of the graduated Sceyrah in Tratalja, which meant that the City would be safe in case the Blood-eaters managed to make it this far. Agathos was more concerned about keeping the City safe, and himself along with it, than conquering a more remote threat. It pained Agathos to have to agree with Ibn, someone he regarded as his inferior in almost every way, but he had to admit that Ibn's idea solved the stalemate they were experiencing with the King.

"Your Majesty, I see the logic in Ibn's idea. Yes, we can spare one hundred and fifty of the trainees, along with fifty of the graduates."

"Wonderful!" the King indeed looked happy. He had been anticipating a long fight with the High Priests, and the meeting had gone quicker than he had expected. "I will send for them immediately, so that they can be briefed as to the exact nature of the threat, and also given their orders." The King stood up, the War Generals with him, and they swept out of the room, leaving Agathos and Ibn alone at the great table. The great door had barely swung shut behind the monarch when Agathos turned on Ibn, his eyes flashing.

"Are you trying to make me look foolish in front of the King?" Agathos hissed.

"N-no, no," Ibn stammered, intimidated as usual. "I just wanted to help, and thought that using the trainees would give both sides what they wanted."

"You'd better be right," Agathos said, his words like ice, "because if it doesn't work, I will make sure the King remembers whose idea this was." Ibn knew Agathos well enough to believe fully in the threat he'd been given. He mouthed a silent prayer to his ancestors, pleading with them to make this plan work.

Agathos stood up, motioning for Ibn to follow him. "Now that this plan of yours has been adopted, we must decide which of the one hundred and fifty trainees to send. We will go speak with the

Master Trainers in the arena and ask them who they feel could become leaders."

Ibn obediently followed Agathos out of the room and down the spiral stairs. When they reached the bottom, they exited the tower and turned left, walking around its broad base to the opposite side, where the fight circle and training areas were located.

The Masters were unanimous in their unwillingness to part with the trainees.

"They are not ready for battle, they are too young," the Master Swordsman said strongly.

"That may be so, but the King has left us little choice," retorted Agathos, "Of the trainees that are fourteen and older, which ones can you part with?" After thinking for a moment and talking amongst themselves, the Masters reluctantly started giving names, resigned to the fact that they had no choice but to give up some of their students. They were outranked by the will of the High Priests.

"And how about the one called Weyre?" Agathos inquired. "She has been gaining in popularity, which is unbecoming a Sceyrah, so to lose her in battle might actually benefit the Sceyrah in general. Seeing a fellow trainee being regarded with such admiration might give rise to other trainees' dreams of individual fame and prowess."

"You speak the truth," the Master Swordsman agreed. Individuality amongst the Sceyrah was strongly discouraged. "But who knows, she may do us proud in the battlefield. There are few trainees, boys or girls, who are as strong and lethal as she. Of all the trainees, she may be the most ready for battle. We can part with her."

Agathos was happy, Ibn could tell. It was no secret that Agathos, along with most of the priests, wanted the Weyre girl gone. Although her fights brought a lot of money to the Temple treasury, her individuality was seen as a much greater liability than the money she could earn for the clergy. Armed with a list of names, Agathos and

Ibn began rounding up the trainees that would compose the leadership of the army that would march against the Blood-eaters.

* * *

Lilija was shocked, more than she could say. Agathos had found her in the arena and taken her aside, telling her to gather her things and report to the Generals immediately. She was going to war. She ran to her cell, collected her few items of clothing, along with her short sword and armor. Her armor consisted of a leather helmet, leather thongs woven on the inside to provide greater strength, with a thin layer of felt for comfort. On the outside, teeth and other bones from various animals like the wild boar provided additional protection. Some of the Sceyrah chose metal helmets when they graduated, but Lilija never would. She liked the lightness and unobstructed view that a leather helmet provided. Besides the helmet she had a thin metal shield, a leather and bone breastplate (again she preferred leather to metal, as it gave her greater freedom of movement), and her short sword. She knew that as a leader of the army she would be riding a horse, and so would need a longer sword as well. That would be provided by the Generals. She also had hardened leather arm and leg bands that offered some protection, especially for her more exposed sword arm. Properly fitted, she ran back outside towards the main arena entrance, to await further instruction.

THE CREATORS

Huracan was furious. The righteous rage that ran through his veins caused what seemed like a fire in his head. His eyes burned, almost causing tears to roll down his cheeks. The tears would come in time, when he mourned, when the sorrow overwhelmed him, but for now there was no time for weeping. Kallos must be caught.

He had felt it the moment the shadow had been released. They had all felt it. But for some reason the three with Kallos had been silent. And then Huracan had known why. They were asleep, the deep sleep from which one doesn't wake. Mortals called it death, but Huracan had only known one of their kin to ever fall asleep, and it was not by an act of volition on the sleeper's part. Huracan had put that one to sleep himself, with violence.

Aiyana, Huracan's lover and consort, had told him immediately of her concern when the shadow was released. It had reminded her of another shadow, a long time ago. At first Huracan had dismissed her concern, a mistake he vowed never to make again. Aiyana had been right. This shadow was different than that other shadow from time immemorial, the shadow Huracan had killed.

That first shadow had been Huracan's best friend, his brother, the one they called Light. He had been beautiful, the bringer of light to many worlds. But then he had begun to speak of his growing desire to raise himself above all others, even their Mother! The shock of such a desire, and the way it unfolded, still made Huracan shudder, and he felt the sorrow again as if it had happened only moments ago. Huracan had found his friend, the bringer of light that had released a shadow, and Huracan had killed him.

And now Huracan was once again called upon to hunt for a shadow. But this time things were different. Kallos hadn't simply unleashed a shadow, Kallos had become the very shadowy evil that he had committed. Huracan knew this almost as soon as he reached the world that the four had created. Something was wrong with this world, or perhaps not wrong so much as different than any world he'd visited before. The world teemed with life, and already Huracan could see the beginnings of different species and races developing in concert with the plants and bugs and valleys and hills. The waters teemed with life also, from the rivers to the oceans. But everything seemed touched by both shadow and light in ways Huracan had never seen before.

And then he saw them, and he nearly staggered from shock. Eluthuria, Karris, and Ugappe! They were there, right in the midst of the things they'd made! Everything he looked at somehow contained these three Creators, from rocks to trees to animals to the first peoples. Some had less than others, so that he could tell just by looking which animals and peoples would soon develop extraordinary abilities, and which ones would not. But they all reflected some aspect of the beauty and power of the three that filled them. It was the fourth, the shadow, that lay like a thin blanket on everything, that made Huracan's heart break even as his blood began to boil. He hated evil, and he wanted nothing more than to defeat

this new foe that threatened the beauty of this novel and wonderful place.

It became obvious as he looked more and more into the natures of these newly created things that Kallos had betrayed the other three, in particular the one they called freedom. Eluthuria had been stripped of her power in an act too terrible to fully comprehend, at least for Huracan. As he absorbed all the knowledge he could from this new world, Huracan learned just how evilly Kallos had acted, by killing the one he loved so that he might feed his own lustful love for himself. Kallos had tried but failed to create his own world within a world, a reality that would have given him everything he wanted without needing him to give up anything he desired. Thanks be to their Mother that Kallos had failed in this. But Kallos was still here, somehow, trapped in this place. Huracan could feel it, could feel Kallos around him, and yet he could not find him.

Huracan's sadness once again threatened to overwhelm him. For Huracan, whose heart was pure, the thought of this great evil weighed heavily on his spirit. So he began to do the only thing he could, in the face of this cold and naked darkness, this shadow that lay just beyond his reach. He began to hunt.

10

THE CREATED

It was still cold outside, but Ari felt like his body was on fire. After decapitating Brynhildur, the blood lust that had descended on Ari remained, and he wanted nothing more than to kill another Blood-eater. In his mind, his rage fueled his imagination so that instead of seeing a ring of savage warriors, he saw a ring of Sceyrahs, the hated City assassins, and he wanted to kill every single one. The circle of warriors had fallen back after Ari's startling victory, and now they stood with their heads slightly bowed, all of them in fear and awe of this strange young man, this boy, who had so swiftly and viciously killed their chief.

One of the warriors nearest to Ari gestured towards Brynhildur's sword, which lay half-buried in the bloody snow near the head-less corpse, saying, "The sword is now yours. You will lead us into battle as our new chief." Ari took in the words without replying, his scarred face remaining impassive while his eyes burned. The heat coming off his body seemed to concentrate in the extremities, especially his sense organs. It was as though the lust that had consumed him gave power to every part of his body that would be needed in

a fight. He felt a strange desire to tear someone to pieces with his hands, and he looked down at his fingers, half expecting his nails to be replaced by long sharp claws like the Weyre. He glanced from the warrior to the fallen sword, and without a word he stooped down and picked it up.

It was a beautiful weapon. Lighter than any sword he'd held before, it was perfectly balanced. He experimented with its weight, twisting the blade back and forth. It responded with precision. It felt good to hold something so wonderfully made. Ari liked the feeling it gave him, the feeling of mastery, the feeling that he was quickly becoming something other than the frightened boy who had fled his village mere days ago. The warrior who had gestured at the sword and who had spoken to Ari remained standing near Ari, as though he needed to say something further. Ari looked at him, raising his eyebrows as he did so. The warrior spoke again.

"We have been planning on raiding south of the river's bend. There are other war parties of Blood-eaters who will meet us at the river's turn, and we were going to travel south, raiding the more prosperous villages that populate the river's banks. Will you lead us?" It seemed that the warrior had considered the fact that Ari may not want to lead, and that having the position of chief thrust upon him could backfire. Ari could simply refuse and leave, and right now no one looked willing to try and force Ari to do anything. So the warrior humbled himself enough to ask Ari if he was willing to do what the Blood-eaters' customs demanded.

Ari thought for a moment. Just a short while ago he'd wished that the Weyre had returned and killed all these savages, but now he had the opportunity to become their leader. The thought was staggering in its own right: he was merely a boy of fourteen, not a seasoned warrior capable of leading a tribe into battle. And yet the idea appealed to Ari more and more. He'd gotten a taste of the blood lust, and he liked it. He was rapidly changing. He felt less and less like a boy, and more and more like a massive warrior, a savage in his own right. Perhaps the gods, if indeed they existed, had led him to this tribe for just such a time as this. Perhaps it was his destiny to leave behind the simple hunting and farming village life he'd grown up with, in exchange for a life of war. He should have been alarmed at his taste for blood, but he'd lived too long in fear in too short a lifetime for self-reflective thoughts to get the upper hand.

He had grown to hate the people who had exiled him from his village, and he hated the City who had ordered his beloved Grandfather to be murdered, the City who worshiped the gods and did nothing to stop such evil. Perhaps now he had the chance to become a skilled killer just like the assassins, the Sceyrah; and with such a set of skills, backed by his growing physical power, he could exact revenge on everyone he hated.

"Yes, I will lead you." Ari's reply seemed to satisfy the warrior, as well as those in the circle closest to Ari. They began to disperse, making ready to break camp and continue their trek through the woods whenever Ari gave the word. Ari found his own pack near the tree where he had been strung up only moments ago. It had been emptied, plundered by one or more warriors. His bow, arrows, and blade were gone. Such highly prized items would have been snatched up quickly. The book, parchment, quill, ink, and clay pot containing Grandfather's remains were scattered in the snow near the empty pack. It angered Ari to see these precious items, especially his Grandfather, reduced to the status of refuse. He felt his blood heat up as he quickly gathered his belongings and stuffed them back into his pack.

As he was doing so, a young, shame-faced warrior approached, fear in his eyes. He held Ari's weapons. He hurriedly placed them at Ari's feet, mumbled an apology, and scampered away. Ari contemplated exacting revenge on this thief, not only for the thievery

71

but for the grievous treatment of his grandfather. But he resisted, once again feeling the blood lust slowly dissipate. It seemed that this lust could settle on him quickly, and leave just as quickly too. It would take some getting used to. Ari decided he needed to talk to that other warrior, the one who had spoken to him. He wasn't exactly sure what was expected of him as Chief, and it couldn't hurt to rely on a seasoned warrior who knew his own people better than Ari ever would. Besides, Ari clearly remembered what had happened to his own father. The position of Chief was not necessarily a life-long position. A tribe or clan could overthrow their leader if they agreed as a group to do so. It would serve Ari well to gain a few allies.

Ari found the warrior, who was busy organizing the melee of other warriors, mixed with women and children, who comprised this nomadic war-mongering tribe.

"What is your name?" Ari asked as he approached.

"I am called Bryndul."

"Bryndul, I am Ari. I have never traveled this far south and east from my village, therefore I will need some help before I can give direction to this tribe. How far are we from this rendezvous you spoke of, the river's turn? And what is the best way to get there?"

"It is at least a two days march, maybe three. I have only been this way once, when I was a child, but I have heard the way described many times by my father. There are a few older warriors among us who have come this far, and they have confirmed what I have been told. We need simply follow this game trail that we are on, and it will lead us to the river's bend. Beyond that, we will rely on our scouts to go ahead of us, as the lands south of the river's bend are not familiar. All we know is that there are villages, and they are wealthy. The river serves as a main trade route. Many boats go up and down, bringing goods from the City to the villages,

and the villages send their wares back to the City." Ari thought for a moment, then nodded.

"Good. Thank you, Bryndul. As soon as the people are ready, we will continue the march." Bryndul acknowledged this with a slight bow, then turned and began giving orders.

Ari noticed that despite Bryndul's assurance that the way was known, four scouts were still sent out, one in each direction. Probably not to find the best way forward or to familiarize themselves with the surrounding territory, but to make sure they weren't being followed or walking into a trap. Despite his own prejudices, Ari began to admire the efficient military manner with which these savages conducted themselves. They left nothing to chance, despite their large numbers. Who could possibly follow them or ambush them was beyond Ari's figuring, but nonetheless he was glad to know that they would be warned well in advance of any threat, from before or behind. Or from their flanks, for that matter. It turned out that the only threat was indeed from their flank, from the forest directly to the north.

Ari and the Blood-eaters marched for two days, and during that time the scouts reported that the countryside seemed deserted. Animals were slowly becoming more plentiful, but there was no evidence that any of the Clans were hunting or traveling in the near vicinity. One of the scouts, the one sent north of the trail, reported the only threat. Weyre tracks. When he told Ari and Bryndul that the tracks were fresh, and that the cat seemed to be keeping pace with the tribe's progress on the trail, there was fear in his voice. Clearly he was spooked at the idea that such a massive predator was keeping itself so close to the tribe. And the scout didn't seem too thrilled at the prospect of continuing his reconnaissance north of the trail. Ari allowed him to remain with the tribe, since they were close to the rendezvous and none of the other scouts reported any threats.

Bryndul seemed curious after the scout had finished giving his report. A few times he almost spoke, then thought better of it. Ari could guess at his curiosity. It was highly improbable for a Weyre to be this far south, and since Ari had been found on this trail, wounded, surrounded by the unmistakeably large paw prints of the deadly cat, this Weyre that kept pace with them could only be the same cat that had attacked Ari. Bryndul would want to know how Ari had survived, and why this cat would now be following them. For now it might be better to foster some mystery, Ari thought to himself. He would allow people to imagine just how powerful Ari must be to not only defeat a great Chief like Brynhildur, but to also repel the attack of a Weyre.

After the second day of marching, they stopped to make camp for the night. Ari decided to try and read the thoughts of the cat that prowled to the north. This connection that he seemed to have with the cat could be useful, and if he could foster that connection and make it stronger he hoped to be able to understand how best to use the connection. He sat by a fire with some of the other warriors, and as they settled in for the night, Ari began concentrating his thoughts on the dark forest.

As the night grew colder, more warriors and family units lit fires, and the soft murmur of conversations mingled with the light smoke and heat of a camp at rest. Those who found themselves a bit further away from the fires collected furs and bundled up for the night. For a while, Ari was distracted by some of these bundles of furs that writhed and shook with a kind of rhythm. He imagined the couples underneath them that were pursuing the more pleasurable methods of keeping warm in the cold winter night. He strove to ignore this other kind of lust, pulling his thoughts back to the forest and away from the sensual piles of furs.

As he focused on the forest, the murmurs of conversation dimmed, and his ears began picking up the sounds beyond the

camp. Wind whistled through the trees, the mournful hoot of an owl echoed somewhere to the south, and in the north, Ari enjoyed the blue-green light display that flickered across the black sky. Stars rose to join their tiny lights to the panorama. And as he watched and listened, he began to feel the forest itself. The soft snow underfoot, the scratch of pine needles brushing against him as he wove through the trees.

With a start, he realized that he wasn't feeling snow through his feet, but through paws. Then he began to see a vision of trees, snow drifts, and pale shadows. He was approaching a particularly large tree, with thick boughs weighed down by snow. He saw two massive white paws stretch out in front of him and begin to dig at the snow piled at the base of the tree. The Weyre was digging itself a small patch of shelter underneath the lowest overhanging branches of this large pine tree, and once satisfied, the cat wriggled itself underneath the scratchy branches and settled in for the night.

Ari realized that his eyes were closed, and the conversations had stopped. Everyone was either asleep or reveling in post-coital bliss. The camp was quiet, the fires dying down. He opened his eyes, amazed at what he'd seen. This connection was greater than he'd realized. With a bit of concentration he'd entered the Weyre, he'd been able to see what she could see, feel what she could feel. Her thoughts, however, were closed off to him. Perhaps he needed to be closer to her. This was something he wanted to pursue, and in time he knew that he would. But for now, sleep began to steal over him and he gladly embraced it, curling up underneath his furs. His last thoughts before drifting off were of the Weyre.

The next morning Ari awoke to find that everyone had already begun to break camp. Once again Bryndul seemed to be in charge, organizing everyone into groups, just as he had done the previous two days. Ari and some of the warriors would lead the tribe, the women and children, accompanied by some of their husbands and

the older warriors would follow, while the remaining warriors would bring up the rear. Ari quickly packed his belongings, tying some of his furs to his pack while wrapping the rest around himself. He shouldered his bow and slung his new sword onto his hip. Before they had begun their march two days ago, Bryndul had presented him with a beautiful leather scabbard. It belonged to Brynhildur, he informed Ari, and belonged with the sword. It was strong, made of hardened leather and attached to a wide leather belt by bits of bone and sinew laced tightly to its mouth. When he put it on and slid the sword into place, he hardly noticed the weight on his hip. It fit so closely to his body that his outer garments fit easily over top, hiding the sword from view. Once again he felt admiration for this weapon as he strode to join Bryndul and the other warriors at the head of the tribe's procession.

With a look to Bryndul that said, "Let's go," they began the last leg of their march. After only one hour, the advance scout returned at a run. He'd met a scout from one of the other Blood-eater tribes already encamped at the river's bend, and the news wasn't good.

"Chief," he said, looking to Ari, "the scouts of our brother tribes have reported seeing horse-mounted scouts from Tratalja near the river's bend. A war party was sent out to try and kill the City's scouts, but their horses are fast and our brothers were unable to catch them. Our brothers fear that if the City learns we are gathering in force to raid south of the river's bend, they will send their army against us."

Bryndul had stiffened at the news, looking alarmed. He spat on the ground and muttered, "May the gods protect us."

"The gods are dead," Ari replied. "Don't waste your words on them." Bryndul looked startled and somewhat upset at Ari's stiff pronouncement. But Ari's mind had already begun to take another track. He was thinking about the City, and a plan began to form in his mind. A plan that, if the other tribes agreed to it, could put a

serious dent in Tratalja's military might. He hadn't thought much about the City and its military forces, especially its hated host of Sceyrah, since his Grandfather's death. But now he did, and the more he thought, the more he became convinced that his idea had merit. He needed to mull it over, allow his initial excitement to wane so that he could better discern his plan's worth.

"For now we have nothing to fear from the City. If they do send their army it will be at least a week before we see any sign of it. We will continue on to the rendezvous and I will meet with the other chiefs to decide what we should do." Ari's answer was met with obedience, as the scout bowed slightly and turned back to the trail he'd come from. Ari wondered if Bryndul was assured by his words. It seemed strange to Ari that a warrior as big and strong as Bryndul could be afraid of anything. But then Ari had no experience with the military might of Tratalja, beyond a single Sceyrah's assassination of his Grandfather. Perhaps the City was a bigger threat than Ari could comprehend.

Within the hour they'd arrived at the river's bend. Ari was awed by the sheer numbers: there must have been at least four thousand warriors camped on the river's eastern banks. There weren't many women and children, so it looked as though Ari's tribe was one of only a handful that were looking for new territory within which to camp for the season. This meant that most of the Blood-eater tribes must be experiencing better hunting than Ari's tribe. As Ari and Bryndul led the way, they were approached by a contingent of senior warriors. Judging by their somewhat elaborate appearances, most, if not all, were Chiefs.

One of them, an exceptionally large and bald man with tattoos inked on his scalp and face, approached Bryndul and grasped his arm in greeting. After exchanging the customary words between Blood-eater tribesmen, the warrior asked Bryndul where Brynhildur

was, since he'd been looking forward to getting re-acquainted with his old friend.

"Brynhildur was killed in a contest. This is his victor, and our new Chief. His name is Ari." Bryndul turned to indicate Ari, who stood silently at his side. The large bald Chief looked at Ari, incredulous.

"Him?? Is this a joke? Brynhildur weighs twice as much as this whip of a boy. Enough of this jesting, I am here to bring your Chief with us to an emergency council."

"It is no joke. Ari is our chief." Bryndul's voice was quieter, and Ari could see that he was uncomfortable. Perhaps he feared this Chief's wrath. For a moment Ari felt for Bryndul, understanding what it was like to bear the brunt of a stronger person's rage. This time, the bald Chief didn't respond right away. Instead, he looked Bryndul in the face long and hard, until Bryndul glanced down, embarrassment and a hint of fear marking his downcast eyes.

"We have come to take your Chief with us to the council," announced the bald Chief whose name was Gol, "but since you have no Chief we will take Bryndul, the brother of Brynhildur, to act as your representative." Gol barked out his pronouncement above the heads of both Ari and Bryndul, making it clear that he was displeased to find a leaderless tribe but he was willing to make this magnanimous gesture anyways.

Ari took away two things from Gol's short speech. One, Bryndul was Brynhildur's brother, which surprised Ari greatly. He had never felt any animosity from Bryndul, despite the fact that Ari had killed his brother. Perhaps Bryndul was as honorable as his words suggested, when Bryndul had spoken of following custom. And two, Ari had just been set aside as Chief by this Gol character, and unless he did something quickly, no one would take him seriously as a leader. He would have to prove himself to the other Blood-eater tribes if they were to accept him. Right now, all they saw was

a boy, not even a warrior, let alone a Chief. Ari's next move proved nearly disastrous.

"Wait." Ari spoke loudly. "You lie when you say we have no Chief. I am Chief, just as Bryndul has said."

"You dare call me a liar??" Gol's voice was much louder, and filled with contempt. "You are nothing but a boy, and a Clan's boy by the look of you, not one of us. How dare you claim to be Chief! If it's true you killed Brynhildur, you must have done so by weeping and shitting yourself in fear, and Brynhildur laughed so hard he tripped and fell on his own sword." The other men with Gol laughed at this, casting disparaging looks at Ari. "If you weren't a boy, I'd already have taken your head for such insolence," Gol continued. "Keep silent if you want to live."

Ari felt his calm demeanor fade as his pride was pricked, and his growing self-confidence quickly evolved into a mad desire to rush at this stranger and hack him to bits.

"You will accept me as Chief and take me into your council, or you will die." Ari's reply had the effect of poking a rabid dog. Gol wheeled on Ari, the back of his hand striking the boy full on the face, knocking him off his feet.

"You fucking runt, you motherless foot-licker!! You dare challenge me to a contest??" Ari quickly picked himself up off the ground, and as Gol threw a second punch, Ari side-stepped the blow and threw one of his own, catching Gol on the left temple. The massive Chief staggered backwards, shock clearly written on his face. The force of Ari's punch was more than what he'd expected from a mere boy. But the look of shock lingered less than a second, and quick as a cat Gol pulled his sword out of its scabbard, and almost as quickly a circle formed as warriors from Ari's tribe and the warriors who accompanied Gol formed the traditional arena for a contest between the two fighters.

Ari began to get the feeling that this fight might not go as easily as his previous challenge. For one thing, Gol was larger than Brynhildur had been, and he was definitely faster. Ari barely had time to draw his own sword before Gol was on him, thrusting his sword towards Ari's stomach with breath-taking speed. Just as quickly, Ari blocked the thrust, but before he could counter, Gol had already spun in place, whipping his sword around in a vicious slash that would have taken off Ari's head. Ari barely had enough time to duck, and before he could regain his position, Gol lashed out with his left foot, knocking Ari onto his back.

Ari tried to raise his sword in defense as Gol pounced on him, but Gol had anticipated that by landing with his left foot on Ari's right forearm, pinning his sword arm to the ground. As Gol jabbed with his sword at Ari's neck, Ari had no choice but to block the blow with his left arm, and the blade bit deeply into Ari's arm, nearly severing it at the shoulder. Ari screamed in pain, and the blood lust that had fueled his challenge of Gol now cooled into a calm realization that death was near. Despite his pain and increasing fear, Ari plotted one last desperate move. With all the strength he could muster, he heaved his right arm upwards, lifting the massive Chief's left leg, and with a twist he aimed his blade at Gol's left side.

Bellowing, Gol staggered back, blood spewing from a chunk of flesh that now dangled from his side like a freshly butchered steak. Ari scrambled to his feet just as Gol once again attempted to deliver a fatal blow, and Ari deflected the thrust with his own sword, and the two warriors once again faced each other.

Ari's side was soaked in blood as his left arm dangled uselessly, and Gol now had a similar stain spreading down his left side. They circled each other warily, each one knowing that the next move could spell the end for either of them. Once again Ari allowed his blood lust to come to a boil, and he felt his right arm shake with a

surge of strength. He wanted nothing more than to tear this man to pieces. It seemed to Ari that Gol slowed, his steps becoming more ponderous. Ari's eyes took in every detail, from the beads of sweat on Gol's forehead to the tiny flakes of snow that had begun to fall.

And then it seemed to Ari that he could smell Gol's blood. The sweet coppery smell drove him wild, and he took in every ragged breath and muscle contraction his opponent exerted. It felt like Ari could hear everything, see everything, with perfect clarity. Ari lunged, swinging his sword at Gol's head. Gol blocked Ari's sword but failed to block Ari's front kick that seemed to instantly accompany the sword's flight, and Gol found himself on his back; and in a reversal of fortunes, Ari was now on top of Gol. But unlike Gol's earlier domination of Ari, this time Ari was quicker.

Before Gol even had time to move to defend himself or scramble out of the way, Ari had leaped forward and plunged his sword deep into Gol's neck, the blade punching straight through and pinning Gol to the ground. The shocked look on Gol's face was fleeting, quickly replaced by the glassy stare of the dead as his head lolled to one side, nearly decapitated. And as Gol's blood spurted out of what remained of his neck, Ari eagerly bent down and clamped his mouth on the side of the gaping wound, sucking at the blood. The circle of witnesses seemed to flinch in unison. Even for Blood-eaters, this proved to be a savage sight.

As Ari took his fill of the warm blood, it seemed that he momentarily left himself and became something completely other, an animal, devouring a kill. As quickly as this feeling came, it left, and Ari pulled back, blood dripping off his face. He pulled himself up, staggered slightly, then sheathed his sword. He felt drunk. He looked around at the shocked faces of those in the circle, but instead of feeling shame, he felt the exhilaration of victory. Bryndul stepped forward, hesitatingly. "Let me see to your arm."

"No," Ari growled, "leave me alone." Without saying another word, Ari turned and walked through the circle of on-lookers, heading north. The exhilaration that he felt was accompanied by a feeling of being utterly alone, which is exactly what he wanted right now. He knew, however, that his left arm was useless, nearly falling off of his body. It would take a miracle if he wanted to save it, and there was only one possible source of such a miracle that Ari knew of. And so he went into the forest in search of her, hoping against hope that she would be able to save his damaged limb.

11

The Sceyrah trainees who gathered with Lilija were instructed to meet the Master of Weapons at the City's armory, to be outfitted for battle. Lilija was already wearing her leather armor, but most of the trainees would prefer the metal armor the City provided. Lilija had collected her pieces of armor from the stock of leather armaments used by the Master Swordsman for their training. Whenever they sparred with weapons, all trainees were required to wear protection.

Lilija did procure one additional piece of weaponry, the long sword she would need once astride a horse. But she didn't need to go to the armory for that; instead, the Master Swordsman had given her his own sword, much to her surprise. He had not seemed reluctant to part with it, rather he seemed worried about her. Perhaps his gift was meant to assuage his own fear for her safety, for if she was equipped with the best sword, this meant that she would have an advantage over any opponent who possessed a lesser weapon.

It surprised and strangely warmed Lilija to realize that this man cared about her. She had always sensed that he took a special delight in training her, but she had always assumed this was because of her exceptional skill. Now she started to think that maybe his attentions went beyond his admiration for her skill. The thought made her blush. Although she was only fourteen, women in the City were usually married by the age of sixteen. The Sceyrah rarely married, preferring to take sexual partners here and there without ever committing themselves to any one in particular. Lilija herself felt strangely separate from these desires, until she found herself thinking about the Master Swordsman.

She shook herself, determined only to think about the upcoming battle and her role in it. The Master Swordsman was much older than she. Besides she was too young to be thinking about such things, or so she told herself. She followed the other Sceyrah, who were being directed to the Sceyrah's Tower after they had been outfitted at the armory. At the top of the Tower was a large circular room, overlooking the City with wide windows on all sides.

When the Master Sceyrah entered the room, his Krayven was perched on his shoulder. It was rare to see a graduated Sceyrah without his or her large black bird, so the sight was hardly abnormal.

"Fifty of you have been chosen to lead Tratalja's army, along with the Generals," the Master spoke. "Each of the Fifty will be in charge of one hundred soldiers, plus two more Sceyrah. There is a further contingent of fifty graduated Sceyrah who have already left on horseback to confirm the reports of the scouts and to devise battle plans accordingly. You will report to them when you rendezvous on the Plains. In order to help you in your task of leading troops and fighting in large numbers, the fifty I have chosen to lead will receive their Krayvens. This is a great honor, usually reserved for your eighteenth birthday, however we have decided that this should be done now. A Sceyrah has never gone into battle without a Krayven, and there is no reason to stop that tradition now."

Lilija's heart began to race. Her own Krayven! She had always admired these fierce black birds, and longed to have one of her own. They were birds of prey, trained to obey the Sceyrah. It was said they could guide a Sceyrah in battle, although Lilija had no idea how they did that.

"The fifty I have chosen, follow me. You will each meet individually with the Oracle, and she will bond you with your Krayven." On

hearing this, Lilija's racing heart ran cold with fear. The Oracle?? She had no idea that it was required to meet with the Oracle in order to receive a Krayven. Lilija knew all too well where the Oracle was located. Deep underground, beneath the Lord's Tower, the very center of the entire Temple complex. As a little girl, Lilija had accidentally gained entrance to the dark tunnel staircase that led directly to the underground cave that housed the Oracle.

Years ago, when she was still trying to memorize all the different underground passages beneath the Temple complex, she had become lost in the catacombs under the arena. She was trying to find her way back to her own cell when she'd found the trapdoor. She had wandered into a room that was normally locked, but on this particular day she'd been walking along the corridor when she saw a High Priest burst out of this room, sobbing in fright. He had stumbled into the corridor, tears streaming down his face, his eyes wide and wild with panic. Even as a little girl she'd known right away that this priest had seen some sort of terrible vision, maybe even a ghost. She herself used to have terrifying nightmares, and occasionally even saw horrible spirits or ghosts while awake. Whether they were demons or merely the spirits of the dead, she never knew, but they left her with the same terror that she now saw written across the priest's face.

The priest saw Lilija, tried to compose himself, then half-walked, half-ran past her. In his haste he had neglected to close the door to this room that had so terrified him. Lilija was affected by his fear, but her curiosity had also been piqued. Mustering her courage, she decided to take a quick look into this room. What she saw seemed innocent enough. It was a simple circular room, with an ornate trapdoor set in the floor. This trapdoor was also open, and as Lilija carefully walked towards it, she could see the beginnings of a stone staircase that led down into darkness. It was hard to describe, but something about that darkness filled her with an unknown dread.

At this point, she had hesitated. Her curiosity began to battle with her growing fear. She wanted to see where the stone staircase led, but at the same time the very thought of walking down those stairs caused panic to set in. She had turned back towards the door, deciding to leave this mystery alone and continue trying to find her way back to her cell, when a whisper caught her mind.

She very nearly screamed in fright, thinking that someone or something was whispering right in her ear, but when she whipped around she discovered that she was still all alone. Then she heard it again. She couldn't quite make out the words but the voice, the thought in her head, seemed to be pleading with her. The whisper, if possible, sounded feminine in her mind. It began to sound like a little girl, a little girl like her, a girl in pain and fear. Lilija began to imagine that the voice belonged to a girl trapped at the bottom of those stone stairs, held hostage by the very darkness that scared Lilija. Lilija began to struggle within herself. She was still afraid, and part of her wanted to run away, but something else was telling her to go down those stairs and help the poor lost girl. The fantasy regarding this lost little girl grew in her mind, and Lilija began crying at the thought of this poor creature trapped and helpless. She needed to help her.

Lilija couldn't stand the tension any longer, and she forced herself to ignore her fears, to ignore the desire to run, and she began to inch her way back towards the trapdoor. With each faltering step she gained some sort of insane courage, and her steps quickened until she reached the trapdoor and almost eagerly began to climb down the cold stone stairs. Almost immediately it seemed that everything went black. Still, she continued walking down, step by step, the whispers growing in her mind, her heart beating faster and faster. Each step brought a fresh wave of euphoria and terror, inexplicably combined. As she continued walking down the stairs, blinded by the darkness, she found that she was no longer thinking

about the girl. There was no girl. She knew that now, but it was too late. The whispers had grown loud, demanding, ordering her to continue walking down, down, down.

The last thing Lilija remembered was tripping on the bottom stair, frantically trying to gain her footing on the strange uneven ground she found herself on. Lights exploded behind her eyes as her head hit something solid, then nothingness engulfed her and she remembered no more.

She awoke three days later in the Medicians tower. As her memory came back, slowly at first, she had a foggy memory of being carried along the catacombs, frightened voices surrounding her, one voice in particular standing out. Later she realized it was the High Priest who had unintentionally left the door open to the circular room in his haste to flee the terror he'd found. This priest was babbling to the other priests who were carrying Lilija, and he was saying something about how she was unlawfully in the presence of the Oracle, he never meant to leave the door open, it wasn't his fault, he'd been scared by what the Oracle had told him, and on and on he had jabbered. Someone else hissed at him to shut up.

Now, as she lay in bed, recovering from her ordeal, she tried to ask the various Medicians who tended her head wound what exactly had happened to her in the staircase. She knew she had hit her head, and said as much, but every question she asked was met with silence. Some of the Medicians looked scared, others looked confused, but none of them wanted to talk about what had happened to her. One of the Medicians, despite his fear, whispered to her that she shouldn't talk about it.

"What happened never should have happened. But you're okay now, don't worry about it, try not to think about it," he'd whispered.

"But something happened, after I fell. I can't remember it, but the priest said I was with the Oracle. What does that mean?" As soon as Lilija said this, the Medicians face grew pale, and his

willingness to talk to her quickly evaporated. He straightened, his kind eyes now growing hard, his look telling her that he wanted nothing more to do with her.

All these memories came flooding back as Lilija mutely followed the Master Sceyrah down the stairs of the Tower, and out into the arena. They walked as a group, the Master and fifty trainees, towards the Lord's Tower. Lilija fought to control her panic. She needed all her self-discipline, gained through years of training how to control her mind and body in every way, to keep herself from running in the opposite direction. She kept telling herself that her fears were little girl fears, caused by an overactive imagination and a blow to the head. At the base of the Lord's Tower they were met by a High Priest, the one they called Agathos, if Lilija remembered correctly. He ushered them into the Tower, then closed the massive door.

"Everyone will wait here while I take each of you down in turn, one at a time, to meet with the Oracle." Pointing at Lilija, he said "You will be first. Follow me."

Lilija felt her legs turn to rubber, and she almost collapsed as her knees began to shake. Shame-faced, she steeled herself and followed Agathos down the stairs. At the bottom of the stairs they found themselves in the catacombs, and turning to his left, Agathos began walking down the corridor. As her anticipation grew, so did her fear, but she managed to follow, her body tense, ready to flee at the slightest provocation. And then they were at the door, the one she'd entered once before. Agathos turned to her, an almost malicious smile beginning to curl at the ends of his mouth.

"Follow me, and say nothing. You will not be able to see the Oracle, as she lives in complete darkness. She will speak to you if she wishes, otherwise you will simply stand in her presence until I summon you back up the stairs after the prescribed time, or she releases you." Agathos opened the door, and following him she

walked into the room. The circular room was the same, but this time it wasn't empty. There were fifty cages, each one containing a Krayven. Walking to the nearest cage, Agathos opened its small door and reached in, grasping the bird. He turned to Lilija and extended the bird to her.

"Take your Krayven, don't let it go or it will fly away. Once the Oracle has bonded the bird to you, it is yours to command, and it will stay with you." Agathos still had the slightest expression, of contempt or disgust or simple arrogance, Lilija couldn't tell, but there was one thing that she suddenly knew as she heard him speak. His voice, although controlled right now, held the same nasally pitch, was the same quivering, babbling, fear-filled voice she'd heard as a little girl. The same voice had spoken at her side as she'd been carried along the very same corridor she'd just left.

"It was you, wasn't it, who left this door open? The door I entered, years ago? And it was you I saw that day, crying and babbling like a little girl who'd seen a ghost." Lilija's words had exactly the affect she'd wanted. The arrogant, contemptuous smile vanished. Agathos looked like he'd been slapped, and shame spread across his face. Without another word Lilija took the bird, and with a renewed display of courage fueled by the sense of accomplishment at putting this arrogant priest in his place, and also partly from a desire to appear strong and fearless in front of him, Lilija strode towards the trapdoor. With her one free hand she lifted it and began her descent.

The Creators

By the world's count, using its sun and moon to track days and years, Huracan hunted for a long time. Thousands of world years. The shadow remained elusive the entire time. Huracan realized through the course of his hunt that a thing such as this shadow, this shadow that somehow was Kallos and yet lacked any substance of its own, cannot be found by a substantive thing like Huracan. Unlike the one other time, when Huracan had hunted and fought his former friend, the light-bringer, this new shadow was intricately and completely wrapped up in the former thing called Kallos. The light-bringer had remained himself, even after causing the shadow to be released, because the light-bringer's actions had not coincided with the actions of the three as Kallos' action had been. If not for the three merging with their creations, Kallos would have remained as himself, separate from the shadow his actions had created.

Huracan's hunt had given him a very great understanding of this new world, and a fascination and wonder had grown in his spirit as he observed the mysteries develop all around him. Even though all living things in this world were growing and evolving in much

the same way as any other world, albeit quite a bit faster, they also all reflected their Creators in ways he'd never seen before. This world had power, what would soon be called magic, and this was a direct result of its intimate bond with the three. Huracan knew that the creatures who were yet to exist would rise up and begin to realize their potential, and in so doing they would begin to exercise these powers. As in other worlds, despite their lack of this magic, power also existed. In those places people spoke of power as an evil thing, or as a good thing, and they would do the same here. Magic would come to be seen as evil, because many people would simply be unable to manage the powers that would lie at their disposal. In their fear and ignorance they would attribute these abilities to darker forces, and would begin to hate and fear them even as they hated and feared themselves.

Huracan knew, as they all did, that to call power either evil or good was a common yet fundamental error in understanding. Good or evil are categories that cannot be placed on things or ideas that lack life. Good or evil describe actions, behaviors, ways of relating to other living things, that can only be applied to sentient living creatures. Such creations, like the humans that would grow out of the seeds of life already sprouting, would possess good and evil within themselves as they acted. Their choices, their behaviors, would be good or evil. The power itself was neither good nor evil. It all depended on how that power got used. And they would have something new, something extra that could be attached to their choices and actions. They would share in some of the unique powers of their Creators, some of the magic that ultimately sprang from the ability to create something out of nothing.

Huracan decided to leave, after realizing his hunt was going to remain utterly futile. He would meet with his Mother and with Aiyana, and together they would talk of this place and try to understand it fully, in the hopes of finding ways to help its life to flourish as much as possible, reflecting as much goodness and love and beauty as it possibly could. They would need to help the humans, help guide them as they discovered their abilities, so that they would have the resources to overcome the shadow. As they overcame, they would also grow in their ability to use their powers for good. In so doing, they would finally reach their full potential. They would share in the lives of the gods in ways perhaps never seen before, and their full potential was to realize this sharing, a participation in the very fabric of the universe. To get there would take a long time, and it would have to involve the choices that all bearers of power can make, evil choices as well as the good.

THE CREATED

Walking down those cold stone stairs was one of the hardest things Lilija had ever done. Every step was harder than the last, and as her fear increased, so too did the darkness, until everything was pitch black around her. She couldn't even see any light above her from the open trapdoor. At least she assumed it was still open, unless Agathos had closed it; however, she hadn't heard any sounds above her. This made her think that the darkness she was experiencing was a kind of darkness that went beyond the mere absence of light. The darkness seemed to swallow light, or maybe it was more like a blanket that covered light. Either way, the darkness felt like a physical presence, like something wrapped around her, touching her.

For a brief second, panic set in and Lilija frantically pawed at her face with her free hand, imagining that there was indeed some sort of thick suffocating blanket slowly constricting itself around her, choking and blinding her. The panic subsided as she once again managed to gain control of her wild emotions. The Krayven that she clutched in her left hand seemed scared as well. She could feel its little heart beating a crazed staccato rhythm against its chest. Somehow this was a comfort to Lilija. At least she wasn't alone, even if her companion was as terrified as she was.

The one thing Lilija hadn't expected was the silence. At no point had she heard or imagined any whispers or thoughts being planted in her head. Agathos had told her to remain silent and wait, and that was precisely what she planned to do. She had absolutely no desire to disturb the silence or to grope about blindly in a mad attempt to explore this terrifying blackness. She would stay right at the bottom of the stairs, feet firmly planted, and brace herself for whatever happened next.

It took a full five minutes before Lilija heard anything. This time, just as before, the whisper sounded feminine, but unlike the last time the voice sounded older. It wasn't a little girl's voice. The voice belonged to a woman, and as the whisper grew louder, the tone and pitch of a regular speaking voice overtook the hushed whispering tones that so quickly evoked memories of her child-hood ordeal.

"I remember you," the voice said. "You came to me when I called, despite your fear. But I lost you to that fear." Lilija's heart felt like it had leaped into her throat, and she had to bite her lip to keep from crying out in fright.

"You are different than the others. You possess something they don't have. In discovering who you really are, you will dis-cover your true power. But there are difficult tasks before you, so to accomplish these tasks I give you gifts of power. The bird you have has a name, as do all the beasts who possess our abilities. His name is Tallulah. Once bonded, he will never leave you, and you must always trust his guidance."

As the Oracle spoke, Lilija's fears began to subside, and in their place a growing curiosity, tinged with uncertainty. What did these things mean? What was her own unique power? What exactly

would these difficult tasks be? Surely helping to lead an army into battle was difficult enough, but Lilija had the sense that the Oracle was referring not only to the upcoming battle but to something else as well. Along with these questions, Lilija also began to form an excited anticipation with her bird. She wanted to know what it would be like to communicate with this creature, to receive its guidance. As she thought these things, she began to feel the bond form between her and Tallulah, a loving kind of bond that strangely warmed her.

Tallulah's heart had slowed, and intuitively Lilija released her grip on his body. With a quick flap of his wings and a gentle tug of his talons, Tallulah vaulted onto her left shoulder and calmly perched there, his sharp mind beginning to make itself known to Lilija.

"To you I give one more gift, a gift that few of your kind ever receive. Your Masters sought to render you nameless, as they do all their slaves, but you are different. Your power comes not only from your skill in fighting, but from your birth. Your parents knew this, for they knew the source of their own power. In the end, however, they were forced to give you up. They foresaw this inevitability, and with great foresight they named you and brought you here. The last gift I give you is your name. You are named Lilija."

These last words sent a shock wave through Lilija. She had no idea that she'd been named; she had always assumed that like most of the Sceyrah, she was an unwanted child, abandoned at birth, given up by parents who would never have bothered to name a child they didn't want to keep. The sound of her own name resonated within her, and she felt Tallulah's own heart-beat quicken.

Lilija didn't know what to think at first. She had a name! Then she began to wonder if it would be possible to track down some information, to learn who her parents had been, what their family history was. The Oracle had hinted at her parent's uniqueness, their

possession of some sort of power, that made them different than the ordinary people that populated this City. Lilija's desire for knowledge, for greater understanding of her own past, grew. As these thoughts raced through her mind, the Oracle spoke once more.

"Go now, Lilija. You are ready for the task at hand. Share your name with no one, only the most trusted friend that you may find, for there are those who will betray you. We will not meet again." With these words, Lilija silently thanked the Oracle, wondering if she could read her thoughts. Then she quickly turned and began to climb the stairs. As she reached the trapdoor, she found that it was open, the light once again triumphing over the darkness. Stepping through, she found Agathos standing there, his malevolent gaze telling her that he had recovered from his shame. There was another trainee beside him, clutching a Krayven.

With a slight nod to her fellow Sceyrah, Lilija walked out of the room and strode down the corridor, excited to begin this next chapter of her life. She felt like she'd been reborn, that she had left her old nameless self in that dark cave with the Oracle, and now she was an even more powerful person, no longer a girl but a woman, ready to tackle any challenge set before her.

She reached the stairs leading to the base of the Lord's Tower, walked quickly up their short flight, and emerged into the room filled with the remaining nervous and excited trainees. When they saw her with her bird, many smiled, excited at their own prospect of early graduation. Lilija left their midst, walked outside, and reveled in her newly found freedom. She was not just a Sceyrah, a nameless member of an elite lethal squad destined to do the bidding of this City. She was Lilija.

14

It did not take long before Ari's blood loss began to take a desperate toll on his body. As he walked into the forest in search of the Weyre, he stumbled, then nearly fell. The trees and everything else around him grew bright in his eyes, and a wave of nausea hit him and he reeled, falling against a tree. He held himself against the strong smooth trunk of the poplar, branches pressing against his pale face. His eyes were closed, and he began to pray, directing his thoughts towards the Weyre.

"Please help me, please come find me, I'm dying." He wouldn't know it, at least consciously, but his prayers were answered within minutes. The Weyre found him, slouched on the ground at the base of the large white poplar tree. She sniffed, recognized the smells of the dying, then she leaned closer, sniffing his arm. The left arm, nearly severed, was the source of death. It was still bleeding, but slower than what Ari had first experienced. She bit into the wounded upper arm, sinking her teeth into the torn flesh, feeling the bones. The taste of the boy's blood told her he was dying. The bones told her that the arm couldn't be saved, not as it had been anyways. Then her instincts, or some unbidden thought, told her to do something she'd never done.

She growled, showing her displeasure, but the thought seemed adamant, becoming a growing instinctual desire within her. She obeyed. She bit her own left leg, and blood began to flow. Lifting her bleeding front leg, she held it above Ari's wound, and her blood began to mix with his. Next, she pressed her blood-stained furry leg to Ari's pale lips, then nuzzled his head, trying to get his head to roll so that his face looked up. She was successful, and her blood began to trickle into Ari's mouth. Once she was satisfied that he'd ingested enough, she began to lick his wounds, starting at the shoulder. She licked and licked, the blood coming off easily, the pale skin showing through more and more. Soon his wounds were clean, the skin healing fast. She knew that given just a short amount of time, the arm and shoulder wound would close in on itself, sealing itself off, not allowing any more loss of precious blood. The arm might not work properly, but it would be saved. Then she curled up against Ari, her heat quickly warming his cold pale body.

Ari had the strangest dream. At first he was falling through a tunnel of light, swirling lights, changing colors as they twisted around him. They seemed to make sounds too, like the sound of metal clanging against metal, only perfectly so, creating beautiful melodies. To Ari's ears, who had never visited the City and therefore had never heard the clarion call of the Temple bells, the sounds were magical. They chimed all around him, calling him further into the tunnel. Then, the tunnel ended abruptly, and it felt as though he'd landed on the softest bed he'd ever felt. He was standing in some sort of clearing, although he couldn't make out any trees around him, just a sense that they were there. Everything was hazy, like a thick fog in spring.

The ground beneath his feet was soft, so soft, and it seemed to bend with him, it seemed to move with his movements. So he stood still, not liking the strange uncertainty, the feeling that he might fall if he couldn't keep his footing. Then another prayer was answered, the prayer his heart had been praying without knowing it. He saw Grandfather again. The old man was smiling, standing in this strange foggy clearing, appearing as suddenly as he had on

the trail many days ago. He strode towards Ari, picking him up in a wonderfully crushing bear hug.

Ari began to sob, feeling all his pent up emotions rise to the surface - the fears he had had as a child, all the feelings of rage he'd been experiencing in these few short days, the pang of loss every time he thought of his Grandfather - everything exploded all at once. He cried and cried, and Grandfather cried with him. The purge had its effect, and Ari felt better than he'd felt since he couldn't even remember when.

"I've missed you so much!" Ari cried, still clinging to his Grandfather.

"I know, I know. I've missed you too." Slowly, Grandfather let go of Ari, but still held his arms, looking in his face. "There are things I need to tell you, many things I should have explained to you years ago. Ari, I am so sorry. I could have prepared you better for the trials you have so recently gone through, but I didn't. I allowed myself to hate your Father, which fueled your own hate. I should have tried to make amends with him, but instead I gave up. Your Father's cruelty was a direct result of my own. I have never told you this, but before you were born, when your Father was still a boy, I was a miserable, bitter man. Your Grandmother, my wife, was a woman of power, a witch, and I became jealous. I myself possessed no special powers beyond an insatiable desire to learn words, to read and write everything I could, no matter the risk.

"When I first fell in love with your grandmother, I was young and smitten with her beauty and power. She knew how to write! She could do things no one else in the village could. We were married soon after I expressed my feelings for her, but then I discovered that my own longings for power were not being met. I wanted more than the abilities of a scribe, and I became jealous and bitter towards the very one I loved. I would never possess the powers that my wife had been given at birth. Some things a person can learn, but others

can only be given, usually at birth. She was born a witch, and there was nothing she could do about that, just as there was nothing I could do about my own lack of magic.

"To my everlasting shame, I began to drink, and I became a violent drunk, taking out my own bitterness and perceived failings on those I should have loved the most. Sometimes your grandmother was able to stop me with a word, with her power, but other times she was unable to prevent me from hitting her, and your father. Ari, your grandmother was not killed by the Sceyrah, as you have been told. She committed suicide." At this point, Hrund stopped, and Ari was overcome to see tears in his grandfather's eyes as he shook with grief, with the remorse of a life lived that could not be undone.

"She loved me, the whole time, despite what I'd become; but she knew she couldn't save me. What I'd become, only I could change. Her heart broken, her will crushed, she did the only thing she thought she could do. She hung herself." Grandfather's face streamed with tears, and Ari's heart went out to him, and the two just stood there for a moment, holding each others arms, heads slightly bowed. Ari waited for Hrund to continue.

"Her death changed me, Ari. I hated myself for a long time, but I quit drinking. By this time your Father hated me, and rightfully so. Perhaps my greatest sin was when you were born, and I gave up trying to mend my relationship with my son, to tell him how sorry I was, to beg his forgiveness and seek his love once more. Instead, I chose to love you with everything I had, to foster the kind of bond with you that I gave up trying to forge with your father. I passed on to you my love of writing and reading, believing that you had a natural gift for this sort of thing. I was partly right, in that you took to it naturally and with great enthusiasm; but I failed to see your greatest strengths, your powerful abilities, the greatest being your ability to connect with the Weyre and absorb her strength.

"I also passed another legacy on to you, a legacy of deceit built on burying family secrets, failing to love those closest to you, often because it's so difficult to love and forgive one's own frail self. I failed to love my wife as I should have, I failed to love my son as I should have, and in so doing I failed to protect you from experiencing the rottenness in your heart and mind that comes from feeding bitterness and hate.

"Ari, you must begin to purge your heart from bitterness. Love yourself, learn to take delight in who you are, and learn to love your father, even though he is dead. Don't do what I did: don't allow the pull of evil to stain your heart, to drag you down. Be very careful of the lust that now lives in your blood. You have the makings of a mighty warrior, and this is good. Use it when you need to, but set it aside just as quickly when hate and revenge threaten to destroy you. In your great strength, do not succumb to mindless rage. I love you, Ari, now more than ever before." Ari had begun to fidget, resisting his Grandfather's words. He didn't want to let go of his rage. He still hated his Father, and he always would. It felt good to hate him, just as it felt good to hate the City and the Sceyrah for taking Grandfather away from him. His hate and rage fed him, fueled him, and he was learning to love the feeling of raw power that now flowed through his veins. Hrund could sense the battle going on within Ari, and he simply held his grandson's gaze, hoping that eventually Ari would accept the necessity to love and forgive, to resist bitterness and hatred.

"I love you too, Grandfather," Ari finally said. "But how can I not hate the Sceyrah who killed you, who took you away from me when I needed you most?"

"It isn't easy," Hrund sighed as he spoke, "It will be a long, hard fight. But it is worth it, Ari. It is worth it to fight against the hate that threatens to consume you." Ari listened to his Grandfather, nodded as though he agreed, and then began to speak.

"Thank you for telling me the truth about the past. There is something else, though, that I have become very curious about. The Weyre: do you have a connection with her, too? How is it that she didn't kill me, that she and I can hear each other's thoughts?"

"The Weyre is an amazing creature! Yes, she and I know each other, because she can see me, and senses my good intentions towards you and her. The Weyre has a unique ability to see the spirit world almost as clearly as she can see the physical world. The Weyre shares this ability with only one other creature, the Raptor. These two animals do not differentiate between the two worlds as we do. On the trail, when the Weyre attacked your Father, I intervened, and she saw me and heard my desire for your safety. Then you discovered your unique gift: you can speak to her, and she can hear you and respond. Very few people have ever been able to do what you can do. Only a few of the great Seiors, a few Waodi, and even fewer witches, can hear and speak with these magnificent animals. The Weyre and Raptor are spirit beings almost as much as they are physical beings.

"This is a beautiful connection you have with her. Foster it, use it, but guard it too. One thing I leave with you, a parting gift: every Raptor and Weyre are born with a name, although some may not remember their names as they go through their lives. When you awake, call your Weyre by name. Her name is Vala."

As before, on the trail many days ago, Hrund began to fade, but Ari held himself back, already missing him but knowing he must go. "I love you!" he called out, and he heard the faint response of love as the old man disappeared completely. The bitterness took over as Ari felt the sharp pain of loss, the reminder that Grandfather was dead and would never again be able to live with Ari every day. Ari would never have the opportunity to learn more words and practice his writing with Hrund, and while a part of him simply felt like crying, a much larger part felt like killing. And just

as his grandfather had slowly faded from sight, so too the clearing also began to fade. The strange ground grew hard as Ari began to feel himself drift, then suddenly pulled as if by a strong current in the river he swam in as a child. He awoke and found himself curled up at the base of a tree, a massive warm pile of fur pressed up against him on his other side. The Weyre began to stir, and Ari struggled to get to his feet, reaching for his left arm. It felt strangely heavy, wooden. His right hand found it, and began to explore. It seemed intact; he couldn't feel the open wound that he knew should be there. His skin felt leathery, tight. He felt weak, but very much alive, and his strength was returning quickly. He could feel the now familiar surge of his own blood, the heat, the power that lived within him. The Weyre was now awake and had sprung to her feet, eying him and growling slightly.

"It's okay, I mean you no harm. Thank you for saving me yet again, Vala," Ari spoke aloud, knowing the Weyre could understand not only his thoughts, but also his voice, since it was the words themselves she knew. From what his Grandfather had said, this was a unique gift and bond that the two shared, and Ari doubted whether she would be able to understand anyone else's words, and he seriously doubted whether anyone else would ever be able to read her thoughts the way he could.

Vala stared at him, then Ari heard:

You know my name, as I know yours, Ari. We are the same.

Ari thrilled to hear her thoughts, and what a difference! What he heard was not disjointed brief words, but clear fully formed thoughts! They could talk to each other, like he could talk to anyone else.

"Will you stay with me? I am going to war with my new tribe. Will you fight with me?"

Yes, I will stay and fight with you.

Ari was ecstatic. How strange, to find such a friend as this in such a deadly beast! He reached out instinctively and stroked her head, and he swore that she began to purr. He sensed some embarrassment on her part; perhaps she had never purred before, so he quickly let go, not wanting to embarrass her further. He knew what it felt like to try and make sense of rare emotions. Together, they walked out of the woods, back towards the Blood-eater camp, and towards the inevitable showdown with Tratalja's army.

15

Ari's return, with a Weyre at his side, had an effect similar to that of stepping on an anthill. Chaos. People scattered in all directions, some screaming as they did so, nearly everyone convinced that they were about to be torn to pieces. Ari had to shout to be heard as he tried to tell people that they had nothing to fear. For a minute or two Ari was worried that this would turn into a blood bath, as a few warriors grabbed for their weapons. If Ari hadn't managed to convince them to put those weapons down, Vala would have made short work of them.

Bryndul was pale with shock at the site of his newly made Chief standing side by side with a Weyre, but he had enough sense to see that so long as Ari was there and no one tried to attack the giant cat, the Weyre wasn't a threat. As soon as Ari saw Bryndul he quickly walked over to the stunned warrior and asked him to try and round up everyone and tell them they had nothing to fear.

"They will believe you. Tell them that the Weyre is with me, she will not hurt anyone unless they attack her." Bryndul nodded, and quickly began yelling at those closest to him to stop running and come back. People from the other Blood-eater camps were beginning to wander over, being drawn by the chaos and curious to know what was going on. Slowly, Bryndul and Ari were able to convince enough people to stay, and word began to spread to those who had fled into the woods that their lives were not actually in danger. Soon the news had reached all the tribes camped in the area, and the frustrating chaos of the past few hours proved to be well worth it in the evening.

That evening, the Chiefs of all the tribes called another Council, and Ari was the guest of honor. In place of the condescension that had greeted him when he first arrived at this rendezvous, this time he was treated as royalty. Ari even brought Vala with him to the Council. This was partly due to Ari's desire to use her presence to strike as much awe into the other Chiefs as possible, but also so that Ari didn't have to worry about some foolish warrior trying to kill her in his absence. He didn't want the headache of trying to convince the Blood-eaters that they were safe as they busied themselves with cleaning up the corpses of their loved ones.

Ari kept silent for the majority of the meeting, content to listen to the other Chiefs as they expounded on the threat posed to them by the City. Various theories were proffered as to the size and composition of the army that Tratalja would send against them. Roughly half of the Chiefs wanted to disband this large gathering of tribes and return to the forests that they called home. The other half wanted to remain and pillage at least a few villages before they were forced by the City to leave the Plains and return to their more traditional hunting grounds.

Bryndul had informed Ari earlier that day, as they had been busy rounding up their fellow Blood-eaters and convincing them that the Weyre wasn't going to kill and eat them, that after Ari had killed Gol and walked alone into the forest, the Council had met and argued for hours without deciding anything. Tonight, Ari hoped to change all that. As the evening wore on, those who were on the side of staying and pillaging began to ask that Ari be allowed to speak.

"He is new to us, and young, but he has earned the right to be heard. He killed Gol, and he walks with a Weyre, which by itself is

unheard of," spoke one of the younger Chiefs. "Obviously the gods are with him, and we must hear what he has to say." Many of the others nodded agreement, and even those who wanted nothing more than to break camp and head for home reluctantly agreed.

Ari stood up and began to speak. "It is true that we face a large and powerful enemy. The City's army has many well-trained soldiers, and they will no doubt outnumber us, too. To defeat this enemy we will need to rely on something other than strength, other than numbers. We need cunning. If you will follow me, I will lead you into battle, and we will win. We won't win because we outnumber our enemy, because we do not. We will not win because we are the more skilled at large-scale battles, because we are not. We will win because we are fighting for our way of life. The City wants to expand, and the territory they want is our hunting lands. We must stay and fight, not just for the chance of plundering the villagers of the Plains, but for the chance of stopping an enemy who will never stop lusting for more and more land.

"This Weyre that you see with me has the ability to see beyond what we can see, and she can tell me things I otherwise would never know. Today she has revealed to me that there are six warships sailing up the coast, and they are nearing the cove at Land's Bend, a mere six miles west of here. They will make landfall two days from now. The City thinks to take us by surprise, but we have the chance to turn the surprise back on them. I propose that we set an ambush, capture these six ships, and send some of our warriors back to Tratalja, and we have them sail these ships right into the City's harbor and sack the City itself."

Ari's words caused an explosion of noise. Men began shouting, some in favor, excitement at enacting such a bold plan clearly written on their faces. Others shouted that such a plan was madness, and every last man of them would be killed. When the shouting died down a bit, Ari spoke again, yelling over the other voices.

"Chiefs, listen to me! We cannot stay and think to plunder a few villages and then run. The City is not likely to leave us alone. They will send their armies, again and again, until they feel they have rid themselves of the threat we pose. We have already shown ourselves in large numbers, closer to the City than ever before. This cannot be undone, and the course of action it has set into motion cannot be undone. Let us not settle for half-measures, and let us not run back to our homes like scared little children. We are Blood-eaters. We are fighters."

More of the assembled Chiefs now added their voices in support of Ari. His words had the effect he wanted: their pride was pricked, and their love of battle was inflamed. Perhaps the greatest factor to sway their minds, however, was the realization that Ari was right: the City wouldn't stop hunting them. If they wanted to preserve and strengthen their way of life, they needed to fight, even if it seemed the odds were stacked against them.

"I have a plan. If you will follow me, I will split us up into three groups. The first group will ambush the soldiers as soon as they disembark their ships. They will then dress in the City's armor and sail those ships back to Tratalja. So long as the harbor masters don't suspect that anything is wrong, they will allow the ships to sail right into the harbor. By then it will be too late for them, and our warriors can enter the City and attack.

"The second group will engage the City's army on the Plains. As soon as the army begins to win, this group will fall back and flee into the forests. The army will naturally pursue, but their effectiveness as a massive unit will be diminished within the trees. They are trained to fight large battles with other large armies. Once inside the forest, the battle should turn in our favor. While this battle is going on, the third group will follow the river valley towards the City, to bring reinforcements to the first group, who by this time should be within the City walls. We can keep our women

and children, along with a small contingent of warriors, safe in the river valley just south of this encampment. The river valley is fairly deep at this point, and should keep everyone hidden. Also, we need to make sure that none of the army's mounted scouts are able to ride back to the City to report on the status of the battle, and we definitely don't want the City to be able to send word that we have attacked Tratalja itself. So I propose that within this third group we leave the few horses we have, with the best riders we have. Their sole job will be to attack the supply lines that trail behind the army and that provide the scouts with fresh horses for riding back and forth from Tratalja."

Much of Ari's plan had come from talking with Vala. She in turn had been talking with Grandfather, as well as other spirits who had appeared to her in recent days. These spirits knew of the City's plan, and had seen the ships sailing up the coast. They also knew how the military would behave, and the information they provided Ari through Vala helped him formulate his own plan of attack. His plan inspired many of the Chiefs, and by the time the evening's council ended all but two of the tribes committed themselves to follow Ari. Those two tribes began breaking camp right away, planning on heading back immediately to their traditional hunting grounds located directly to the north.

The next day the Chiefs met again, and this time they divided their warriors into three groups. Ari and Vala would remain with the main group that was designated to engage the army on the Plains. Bryndul was put in charge of leading the ambush on the six ships. The final group was led by an older Chief named Brystol. Bryndul's group quickly armed themselves and began a quick westward march towards Land's Bend, where they would lie in wait near the cove to ambush the City's soldiers after they had left their ships.

Ari and Vala led two thousand warriors out into the Plains, away from the river. Ari sent a few scouts running ahead to discover

exactly where the City's army was, and how long they could expect to wait before meeting them. Meanwhile, Brystol began leading a thousand warriors down into the river valley, to begin their southward march, hidden from view. It took one day for Ari to receive word from the scouts that Tratalja's army was sighted on the Plains. They could expect to engage them the next day. The sobering but not unexpected news was that the City's army outnumbered them at least three to one.

THE CREATORS

Huracan returned with his lover Aiyana, and together they began to implement the plan they had discussed with the All-Mother. As always, words were important, as they represented the starting place of all human sharing. Communication forged connections between the sender and receiver of any kind of communique. The children of the All-Mother shared an intimate connection that transcended simple verbal cues. This level of intimate communication, this sharing of pure thought and emotion that existed outside the space-time barrier, was far beyond most of the mortals in any of the worlds yet created. There were a few isolated cases where humans and animals had begun to share in this level of connection with each other, but this current world was still too new.

Therefore Huracan and Aiyana began where they always began, whenever they taught a new world. This new world needed language, so they taught them the words needed to describe their reality. Soon the first peoples were able to speak to each other, and soon after that they began to write their words down. This was common practice in any world, because people always realized that

simply speaking to each other was a limited level of sharing and connecting. If you wanted to communicate to those who lived far away, or who would live after you, you needed to either memorize and tell stories over and over, or you needed to write them down and preserve them physically. Otherwise you ran the risk of losing what you and your ancestors had learned. Oral traditions flourished for awhile, but Huracan and Aiyana insured that the first peoples began to write as well as recount their stories orally. Eventually the written word would overtake the oral traditions in importance, as had happened in other worlds.

The first books were made from the bark of fig trees, made more elastic by soaking them with the sap from rubber trees, then painted with the starch from vegetable tubers. The final step, after the words had been written, involved painting the pages with colors found in the earth's dirt or with juices from the berries that grew in large bushes. The pages were painted with these colors using soft feathers. The ink that was used to write the words of the first peoples was either made from pressed berries or the treated blood of animals, or in rare instances humans. Then the pages were folded and bound either by strong vines or the leather straps cut from the hides of bears and wolves.

It was in the creation of these books by the earliest human tribes that Huracan and Aiyana discovered the first tangible signs of magic. When certain people, who possessed a greater likeness to the Creators, wrote words in these books, their written ideas began to take on a life of their own. These especially gifted individuals were able to create something out of nothing! Their stories, their histories, their thoughts and desires and feelings, began to take on a reality that affected their physical surroundings and their human communities and relationships.

Huracan and Aiyana marveled at these mysteries, and as they continued teaching these peoples they also began to learn from

them. What they learned was that these peoples had a collective memory, a memory of what the three Creators had done. Their collective memory seemed to end when it came to the fourth, the murderer, however, and this lack of knowledge was something that Huracan and Aiyana chose to reveal to the first peoples. It was Aiyana who spoke to one of the especially gifted persons, who wrote down what she told him. Leaving nothing out, Aiyana told the story of how Ugappe, Karris, and Eleuthuria chose to enter fully into their creations, but their goal was tainted by the murder of Eleuthuria by Kallos. The scribe who wrote the story down chose to do so on a vellum scroll. This was the first time that animal skins were used as writing material, and the animal that was chosen, along with the manner in which the writing was performed, helped to insure that the scroll would last an extremely long time.

It was in this way, this sharing of knowledge, that Huracan and Aiyana learned exactly how the three had merged. The collective memory of the first peoples revealed that the three had written down their desires on their own bodies. These words insured that despite their own sleep, despite their own merging with the world, their desire to seed this world with their very lives would not fade even as their bodies faded. These words were able to take on a life of their own, and in so doing the desire of the three to create something new became a physical reality. Every living thing in this world was able to receive some part, no matter how small, of the very life essences of the three Creators.

At first Huracan had been worried that as humans discovered their abilities to write, and sometimes bring into being the very things they wrote about, the world would be thrown into chaos. Aiyana had to remind him that the same creative desires that flowed through their veins also flowed through the veins of these mortal creations, and these desires were coupled with the same universal sense of harmony and balance. It was simply not possible,

given who and what their Mother was, and therefore who and what all created things everywhere were, for harmony and balance to become so thwarted that a world would devolve into complete chaos and anarchy. Such an unraveling of the very fabric of creation went against every good force of harmony and balance that the creative process always possessed.

Yes, there would be those who would write from a selfish ambition and greed, a desire for power and wealth and fame at the expense of others. Depending on how much magic such a person possessed, their writings could cause untold pain and suffering. But the reverse also held true: there would be those who would write in order to create new and beautiful things. Such writers would never desire to hurt and abuse others in the process of achieving their visions of reality, and they would always rise up in defense of the good whenever an evil person sought to overthrow the balance of things in a lustful pursuit of power. Depending on how much magic these individuals possessed, they would be the cause of great freedom and joy in the lives of those they affected.

Huracan acknowledged the wisdom and foresight of his lover. His fears were ungrounded, whereas her wisdom was built on truth. Together they finished what they had begun, and their plan was now put into place. They would return one day, and hopefully on that day they would see the three as they had desired to be seen, flourishing in the lives of those they'd made in love, the creatures that now walked and lived and talked and wrote together in the woods and plains of this magical new world.

THE CREATED

Lilija's own scouts reported that the Blood-eater army was smaller than they'd been told. According to the scouts, the force that had been sighted just south of the forest was only about two thousand strong. Lilija spread the word to the other Sceyrah, and they made ready for battle. The archers were brought to the front line, and they were closely followed by the cavalry, led by the Sceyrah. Every Sceyrah wore the traditional black cloak over top of any armor they had chosen to wear. Unlike the more elaborate black flowing gowns that the priests wore, the simple black cloak of the Sceyrah was tight-fitting: this helped to insure that it didn't get in the way when the Sceyrah was engaged in battle. The cloaks flared slightly at the waist, allowing for the assassin's sword to remain hidden beneath the cloak whenever the sword was sheathed. But other than that, the cloaks clung to the body. The majority of the army consisted of its infantry, led by the Generals who were on horseback. The next day, Lilija sighted the Blood-eaters through Tallulah's eyes as her bird flew high above the Plains. By midday, the archers were within striking distance.

Ari had given the Blood-eaters strict instructions not to rush ahead until he gave the signal; instead, they slowly walked forward, following Ari and Vala. He could feel the restlessness of his savage warriors, their eager desire to rush this hated enemy, but Ari wanted to wait. He wanted to shorten the distance between the two groups before they rushed their front lines. Ari and Vala were out in front, twenty yards or so ahead of their two thousand warriors. When Ari saw the first volley of arrows being fired, he signaled back towards the Blood-eaters, and they crouched down and lifted their wood and leather shields in front of them.

Ari tightened his grip on his own shield, and awkwardly held it up in front of his face as he knelt on the ground. His left arm, which held the shield, was stiff. It was difficult to move his recently injured limb; it did not respond quickly or easily. Ari hoped that in time it would improve. At least for now, it had the strength to hold the shield, and Ari felt the thud of an arrow as it embedded itself in his shield. Vala was crouched down beside him, growling, her ears pinned back against her head. Ari wasn't worried when he saw her spring to her right side at the last minute, dodging an arrow. With her keen eyes, instincts, and speed, he was confident that an arrow would never touch her. Ari waited for the second volley. His plan was to allow the archers to fire a number of volleys, while the gap between the two groups closed. Once Ari felt they were close enough, they would rush the City's army. After the third volley, Ari gave the signal, and he and Vala began to run.

He heard the shrieks behind him as his warriors began screaming their war cries, and the sound filled him with a kind of unearthly energy. He felt his blood lust begin to grow. He ran faster, and soon after he had begun his mad dash towards his enemy's front line he could see the terror on the faces of the archers as they saw Vala rushing towards them. Some of the archers were frantically trying to notch their next arrow, but many were already breaking their

lines, trying to flee behind the protection of the cavalry. Drawing his sword, Ari ran even faster, and then he saw the archers break ranks en masse, with the cavalry bursting through, galloping towards them.

Soon the air was filled with the crash and clang of metal and men and horses colliding with each other. Ari dodged a massive war horse, slashing upwards as he did so. A scream, and a well-armored soldier fell to the ground, Ari's sword having found the one small unprotected slit just below the breastplate. It was hard to see Vala. The few times Ari caught a glimpse of her, she was a blur, her color seeming to change from white to brown, camouflaging herself by absorbing the colors of the men and horses and brown-green grasses of the Plains that surrounded her. Screams of terror were commonplace wherever she ran, and men were viciously cut down by her powerful strides as she clawed and bit her way through the ranks. As Ari would learn later, the Weyre possess a unique kind of fur. Their hair absorbs light and is then able to reflect back its own surroundings, having a similar camouflaging effect possessed by the chameleons that live in the desert.

Ari fought his way through the cavalry and managed to take down one of the Sceyrah. When he first sighted the hated assassin, he was filled with rage. He had never seen one firsthand, but he'd heard from others that they always wore the black cloak, and usually had a Krayven with them, so he was able to instantly recognize members of the group responsible for murdering his grandfather. Slashing forward, he sprinted towards his mounted enemy. For a very brief moment he felt a twinge, a check within himself, as though a part of him didn't want to give in to the rage he was feeling, but he ignored it as he leaped up and swung his sword. The Sceyrah attempted to block his attack, but his sword flew out of his hand as Ari's strong stroke knocked the assassin clear off his steed. Before the Sceyrah hit the ground, Ari's sword took off his head. At

almost the same instant, Ari saw in his peripheral vision a black streak as a Krayven screeched and flew towards him, its sharp beak and claws meaning to take revenge on the person who had just killed its master. Before it could have its vengeance, however, a flash of mottled fur blocked Ari's view, and the bird met its end in Vala's mouth.

Looking up, Ari had just enough time to roll to his right as another Sceyrah galloped past. He was startled to see that it was a woman, or rather a girl, and she looked to be about his own age. There was a fierce look in her eyes as she reined in her mount and turned to charge at Ari again. If she noticed the Weyre tearing her cavalry to pieces a mere stone's throw away, she didn't seem to care. Her sword was out, and she slashed down at Ari. He blocked, then jabbed, aiming at her side as she rode by. Before he had time to ascertain whether or not his jab had found its mark, the Sceyrah had swung off her horse and slashed at Ari's head. Ari was surprised at her speed and agility, the fluidity of her movements. He was able to bring his shield up to block the blow, but he didn't have time to counter. Over and over her blows, jabs, and thrusts came at him with lightning speed, and all he could do was block.

They fought like this for a few brief moments, until Ari's rage began to take hold once again. He decided to take the offensive, even if it meant exposing himself to harm. With a shout, he smashed his shield towards the Sceyrah's sword arm while swinging his own sword towards her midsection. The skillful Sceyrah spun and brought her sword across her body, blocking Ari's sword, but his shield caught her in the shoulder, knocking her backwards. With a surge of adrenalin, Ari jumped forwards, thrusting his sword towards her chest. Lying on her back, the Sceyrah deflected his sword as she simultaneously kicked upwards, catching Ari in the gut. At the same time, Ari felt a sharp pain in his neck, and he instantly knew that it was her bird, digging its talons into him. Ari

staggered back from her kick, and with a roar of rage he grabbed at the back of his neck, snagging a few feathers as the bird shrieked and flew back into the sky.

The Sceyrah seemed enraged that he had almost killed her bird, and once again Ari was on the defensive as she jabbed at his torso. He felt her sword catch his chest as he spun, trying to avoid its deadly edge. The wound wasn't deep, and again Ari used his shield to knock the Sceyrah back. As Ari and Lilija continued to fight each other, the battle around them was slowly being won by the City, as Ari had predicted. He sensed Vala's rage somewhere nearby as she brought down yet another soldier, and his own lust was inflamed. In the back of his mind, a nagging thought persisted, telling him to fall back.

Now is the time, lead your warriors back to the forest. Fall back!

He didn't want to listen. All he wanted to do was kill this Sceyrah, then kill all the other Sceyrah. He swung madly at Lilija, but once again she deflected his sword and countered with her own swift stab, nearly cutting clean through him. He dodged at the last minute. Her skill was definitely far superior to his own. His saving grace was his speed, his strength, newly gained from the Weyre. He could even anticipate certain moves, see them happen before they happened, and yet this particular Sceyrah proved elusive. It was a stalemate, neither one of them gaining a clear advantage. Finally, Ari began to listen to the thought, and he knew that he must follow his own plan and fall back. As Lilija prepared to deliver another blow, Ari threw his shield at her, catching her by surprise, and then he ran away from her, yelling to the clusters of Blood-eaters that were still ferociously battling the City's soldiers.

"Fall back!" he screamed, over and over, and soon many of the warriors followed him, running on the Plains. The forest was three or four hundred yards away, and Ari knew that this was the most

vulnerable time for all of them. He hated running away, and he hated to see a few warriors fall as their sprint to the safety of the trees was cut short by an arrow in the back. He couldn't see if Vala was with him, although he thought he could sense her somewhere nearby. He could hear the hoots and cheers from the City's soldiers as they gave chase, believing that they had beaten the Blood-eaters and were now chasing a scared rabble of survivors, a disorganized and undisciplined horde. Ari could see many of his warriors already in the trees, crashing through underbrush as they tried to get as deep into the woods as they could.

The plan was to get far enough into the trees to make it difficult for Tratalja's soldiers to spot them. Then, they could turn and fight using quick attacks then falling back, fighting more as individuals than as one big unit. This more familiar style of fighting, combined with the more familiar environs of the forest, would hopefully prove to balance the scales somewhat between the two opposing forces. Ari had no illusions that they would completely defeat this army, but he wanted to give his warriors the best chance at success while providing an easy retreat. At any time they could simply fall farther back into the forest, and eventually the City would have to retreat. The cavalry would find it nearly impossible to follow in the thick trees, and the soldiers would not want to pursue an enemy that they could no longer see.

This all made sense in Ari's head as he ran, but a part of him desperately wanted to turn back and fight, to try and kill as many as he could, especially the Sceyrah. He had to fight within himself to stay the course. Soon he was in the trees, dodging branches, making his way deeper and deeper into the thickening cover. He could hear orders being shouted behind him, although he couldn't quite make out the words. Then there was a mottled greenish brown blur beside him, and he heard Vala's thoughts:

The cavalry has stopped, and the archers also. There seems to be disagreement among them, I sense their confusion: some want to pursue, others are afraid.

He asked Vala to see what else she could learn, and then come back and find him and tell him. He thought he saw her fade away out of the corner of his eye, but it was hard to tell. Spring seemed to have arrived in the last few days, most of the snow was melted, and the color green was once again dominating the trees and ground. Vala seemed to be reflecting the change of seasons, and again Ari marveled at her abilities. She could blend into her surroundings so well it was almost as though she was invisible.

18

Lilija was surprised when the young Blood-eater she'd been fighting suddenly retreated and, along with the rest of the savages, began running towards the forest. She'd first taken notice of the scarred Blood-eater when she'd spotted him easily dispatching one of her mounted colleagues, and she had quickly decided that he was much more of a threat than his youth and size would suggest. She confirmed her suspicions when she started fighting with him. Then, he'd almost managed to grab Tallulah, which enraged her.

From that point on she threw everything she had at this boy, determined to kill him as quickly and viciously as possible. Strangely, nothing seemed to work. He didn't have much skill with the beautiful sword he carried, but she couldn't seem to take advantage of that fact. He either managed to block her blows or dodge them altogether. His own blows were quick and powerful, and for the first time in a long time Lilija felt unsure of success. Then, just when she was really beginning to enjoy the challenge of it all, he fled.

She found a riderless horse and quickly mounted, giving chase while screaming orders to those around her to pursue the fleeing savages along with her. She soon noticed that her army was quite disorganized, and she realized there were very few mounted Sceyrah left. She reigned in her mount, twisting back and forth in the saddle, trying to see who was still left to help her lead the troops. She spotted numerous Generals on horseback, and a good majority of the regular cavalry remained unharmed, but her fellow Sceyrah were few in number. She gave up the chase in order to ride over to the Generals.

"We need to organize the soldiers and give chase," she said once she was close enough to one of the Generals.

"That's what we're trying to do, but we've lost many of your kind as I'm sure you can tell. That wild cat seemed to be targeting them. I saw it tear quite a few Sceyrah off their horses, ripping them apart as it did so." The General seemed quite shaken up by what he'd witnessed. His voice shook a little as he spoke, and his eyes darted back and forth, betraying his efforts to appear calm and in control.

"Gather as many as you can and order them to pursue. It will be harder to find and kill these Blood-eaters once they reach the trees."

The General nodded his assent, and both he and Lilija wheeled their horses and quickly rode off in opposite directions, organizing the soldiers and giving them the order to pursue. The other Generals and the few remaining Sceyrah did the same, and soon the scattered soldiers were once again organized into fighting units. The archers managed to loose a few arrows at the fleeing warriors before they had to stop, not wanting to fire on their own soldiers as the cavalry and some of the infantry were already racing across the Plains towards the trees. The slower Blood-eaters were the unfortunate casualties of this renewed pursuit, and soon the cavalry and infantry were whooping and hollering, shouting cheers of victory as they killed their enemy.

Lilija wanted to find one particular enemy, the young warrior she'd been fighting before the retreat had been called. He was strangely powerful, and she sensed that as a leader he posed a much greater threat than any of the others. She kicked her horse into a gallop, looking for him. Tallulah flew off her shoulder,

wanting to give her a better view. Through his eyes she saw Ari dart into the woods, a strange-looking animal running alongside him. It was hard to see exactly what it was, it blended in so well with the grasses. Once it entered the trees, she lost sight of it and of Ari. She wanted to try and see what was going on in the forest, she wanted to know if the Blood-eaters were really on the run or if they would try and re-group within the forest and attack their pursuers. Her desire to know this kept Tallulah in the air.

Tallulah flew back and forth over the trees, his dark beady eyes glinting in the sun as he tried to penetrate the foliage and track the movements of the enemy. He was able to see flashes of movement, what appeared to be warriors spreading out, running north through the woods. It didn't look like they were organizing for any kind of counter-attack, but Lilija began to get a strange feeling that something wasn't quite right.

She reigned in her mount as she reached the edge of the trees, and she shouted at a few of the Generals, who rode to join her.

"I'm beginning to think that we shouldn't pursue after all. These savages know these woods, and I'm worried that if we chase them they will be able to mount a counter-attack, using the forest as cover. We had the upper hand on the Plains, but we aren't prepared for this kind of fight."

"Has your bird seen something?" one of the Generals asked. The Generals were aware of the special relationship between a Sceyrah and their Krayvens. Lilija hesitated before giving an answer.

"Nothing to suggest that they're re-grouping, but it seems strange that they retreated so suddenly. We were beating them, that is true, but they were still holding their own. I am beginning to suspect that they remained close to the forest for a reason. They allowed us to march to them, and in so doing they chose this particular place to make their stand against us. Perhaps they want us to chase them into these woods."

By now Lilija had been joined by five Generals and five Sceyrah, all of them mounted. Shockingly, it seemed that all the other mounted Sceyrah were either dead or laying wounded on the battlefield. Lilija hoped that some were already in the forest, giving chase. Despite their superior skill, it seemed that the Sceyrah had suffered the greatest losses among the entire cavalry.

Lilija's words had convinced some of her fellow Sceyrah, and a few of the Generals, but the others wanted to pursue and kill as many Blood-eaters as possible. Since they couldn't agree on a single course of action, it was decided that they would split up, with Lilija and two of the Sceyrah riding back to the City with word of the battle's success, while the remaining three Sceyrah and the Generals would continue the pursuit. Lilija found herself muttering a quick prayer to the gods, something she rarely did. She asked them to protect these soldiers, and to give them victory over these hated savages.

19

It was obvious by all the smoke in the sky that something was wrong. Except for a brief battle with some mounted Blood-eaters who seemed intent on stopping anyone from getting back to the City, the past six days of hard riding had been quite uneventful. Now, as they neared Tratalja, Lilija sent Tallulah into the sky to survey the City. What she saw through her bird's eyes chilled her. The City was being sacked. Houses and businesses were burning, there were pitched battles being fought between Blood-eaters and Sceyrah, as well as some battles between the savages and the City's soldiers. Lilija had been wrong. The real trap was not being set in the forest. The real trap was already sprung on an unsuspecting City.

She kicked her horse's flanks with her heels, and she rode towards Tratalja at a gallop, her companions close behind. The City gates were open wide, the bodies of soldiers strewn across the gaping mouth that led into the heart of the metropolis. Lilija and the few who rode with her quickly found a pitched battle being fought between the Blood-eaters and some City soldiers, and with the help that Lilija and her companions brought the fight was soon over. After a few hours of fighting in other small skirmishes, the tide was slowly turning in Tratalja's favor.

"To the harbor! To the harbor!" shouted someone from within the ranks of soldiers gathering to Lilija's right. Immediately the soldiers complied, moving as one towards the waterfront located some blocks away. Lilija followed on her horse, using Tallulah's eyes to get a picture of what was happening on the water. It seemed the Blood-eaters were trying to retreat on one of the ships that had brought them to the City.

Bryndul and the remaining Blood-eaters had barely boarded the ship when he saw the swarm of soldiers converge on the harbor front, and he urged his fellow warriors to quickly grab the oars and get them a safe distance away. Luckily there were only a few archers amongst the soldiers, so Bryndul's men suffered only a handful of casualties as they scrambled to their various positions on the deck. Once they were out of the natural shelter provided by the tall cliffs that flanked the harbor, Bryndul ordered the sails to be unfurled. He was glad to be sailing away from this City, this mass of humanity and military might that threatened him and his people, back to the familiar forests of the north.

Ari's plan had worked. They had ambushed the soldiers back at the Bend soon after they'd disembarked from the ships. After killing all the soldiers, they stripped them of their armor, and very wisely kept some of the sailors alive. They would need them to sail the ships since Blood-eaters were not an ocean-going people. Favorable winds got them to the City within a few short days, and the harbor masters suspected nothing, seeing only men dressed in the City's armor on board the ships, and thereby assuming that they were the same men who had sailed out of the harbor scarcely a week and a half earlier. Once they'd dropped anchor, they disembarked and made short work of the harbor guards. Then they'd begun their rampage, looting anything of value from homes and businesses and then burning everything in their wake.

Bryndul ordered the retreat when it became obvious that the City was winning the war against them, but before he did so he sent two warriors on horseback to intercept Brystol and the reinforcements.

Since the ships had arrived sooner than expected, Brystol's force hadn't arrived at the City, and now they weren't needed. They needed to be told to turn back. Still, Bryndul was very happy with what they had accomplished. They had lots of gold, silver, and other plunder, including weapons and food. They had also captured some women, who would make lovely brides for some of the warriors. Perhaps best of all, they had put a serious dent in the City's ability to mount a counter-attack: they had been able to kill a lot of soldiers.

Lilija was furious. Her first battle, her first chance to prove herself outside of the Temple, and it had all gone horribly wrong. She was gathered with the remaining Sceyrah in the Temple arena, and the Master Sceyrah was there along with the King and his remaining Generals. Agathos the High Priest was also there, and something in his look made Lilija nervous. Then the Master Sceyrah spoke.

"Our City lies in ruins, and we Sceyrah have been seriously disgraced. Never in our history have we suffered a defeat quite like this. It is the opinion of the King, and all of us Masters, that this disaster is rooted in a foolish plan led by weak children. Those who are responsible will be punished. For the time being the offenders will be locked up while we decide how best to punish them."

Just as Lilija was wondering who was going to be held responsible for the sacking of the City, she felt strong hands grasp her arms. Two City soldiers propelled her towards the Master Sceyrah, who met her gaze with cold contempt. As she stood before him, he grabbed Tallulah off her shoulder and wrung his neck, tossing the lifeless body to the cold paving stones at her feet.

"No!" Lilija cried, trying to break free from the guards who held her, but to no avail. Feeling intense shame - as well as sadness at the death of Tallulah - Lilija was stripped of her weapons and armor and taken to the dungeons.

Lilija couldn't believe this was happening. Everything seemed surreal. The cold hard paving stones of the catacombs, which gave way to the rougher stones that composed the winding stairs that led down into the dungeons, were like something out of a dream. She brushed against the wall, feeling the damp cold stones through her thin shirt. It was dark, except for the torch that one of the jailers held in front of him as they descended. They were now quite far beneath the City, in a place few citizens or foreigners ever had the misfortune of seeing for themselves. Soon she found herself locked in a small cell that stank of rotting meat and mold and death. She could hear someone else being led into another cell, and he was pleading with his captors to let him go.

"Please, please, let me go. I don't belong here. It wasn't my fault, I swear." His pleas, however, were met with stony silence as the guards threw him into his cell and clanged the heavy wood and iron door shut, locking him in. Lilija thought she could hear the faint sounds of sobbing coming from his cell, although the walls were so thick that she could barely hear anything even though he was in the cell right next to hers. The initial shock of being blamed for the City's misfortune had worn away, and now she was growing angry.

She knew full well that the reason she was being blamed was because the priests, for the most part, did not like her. Especially Agathos. She began to imagine what sort of punishment they would mete out to her, and her anger grew. It was the injustice of it all! She wished that she had died on the battlefield, at least that would have been an honorable death. What if they executed her? She couldn't bear the thought of dying at the command of a petty jealous priest like Agathos. She paced her cell for awhile, fuming. Then she thought of Tallulah, and her anger turned to sadness, and for the first time in many years she began to cry.

Up above, in the Lord's Tower, the Lord's Council gathered to decide what to do with the prisoners. Agathos was seated at the

table, along with a few other high priests. King Fadel sat at the head of the table with a few of his most trusted Generals. All the Master trainers were present also, along with their leader, the Master Sceyrah, who sat next to Agathos. It was Agathos who first brought up the possibility of executing Lilija.

"As we all know, she has become famous in our City, and I believe it would send a strong message to those who dream of rebelling against us that if you strive to exalt yourself above the City, you will be destroyed. She has brought down the wrath of the gods upon Tratalja. It was foolish of us to allow her to be a part of the army that was sent against the Blood-eaters, that much is certain, and now we are reaping the rewards of such folly. I vote that we execute her at dawn, in the arena, along with Ibn." Ibn was the other prisoner, the one Lilija heard sobbing in the cell beside her.

"It was Ibn's plan," Agathos continued, "that failed to protect the City. Based on his plan, we sent out too many of our soldiers and Sceyrah, and left the City under-protected."

There were many nods of agreement, save for one. The Master Swordsman had frowned the entire time that Agathos was speaking, and once everyone else had expressed their agreement with the High Priest the Master Swordsman spoke up, saying, "Let us not be too rash. The execution of these two will indeed send a message, but not necessarily the one that Agathos envisions. Instead of putting the people in their place, it could serve to anger them and inflame a rebellion. Remember, this particular Sceyrah is popular, very popular. The people love watching her fight, and they love watching her win. If we execute her, we execute their hero."

"Nonsense!" retorted Agathos, his face turning red. "How can we allow her impious and haughty independence to go unpunished?? If we let her go, we are telling the people that it is permissible to go against the natural order of things, to rebel against those of us who lead them by the will of the gods! Then they will

rebel for sure, believing that they have every right to do so! Such a pernicious belief must be squashed before it has the chance to grow." Once again many of those seated at the table agreed with Agathos, but a few began to voice their doubts, showing that the Master Swordsman's argument had been convincing enough to change the minds of at least a couple of them. This led to some heated exchanges as the debate raged over what to do with their two prisoners.

"Enough!" the King bellowed, after a particularly nasty exchange between Agathos and one of the Master Trainers who had come to be particularly convinced that the Master Swordsman's view was correct. "It is time to vote," the King continued, "and as you are all aware, we need to have a majority consensus amongst ourselves before we can proceed. So: who is in favor of executing these two? Raise your hand." The Master Swordsman's face fell as he saw a clear majority raise their hands. Some of them had hesitated before doing so, but after receiving a glare from Agathos, they timidly lifted their hands and joined the majority.

In the end, only the Master Swordsman and two Master Trainers were opposed. It was decided that both Lilija and Ibn would be beheaded the next day at dawn, in the arena. Admission to this event would be free, insuring that as many people as could fit into the arena would be able to bear witness to the City's swift punishment of those whom it had deemed responsible for Tratalja's sacking.

After everyone had left the Tower's upper room, the Master Swordsman remained behind, sitting with his head in his hands, thinking. His love for Lilija, which had been steadily growing over the past few years, now consumed him. He would never have spoken up in the defense of just anyone, but when it came to Lilija he wanted nothing more than to protect and care for her. The thought of her death terrified and angered him. He knew he couldn't let it happen. A plan began to develop in his mind, and after a few minutes, he left the room and made his way down to ground level. Walking out into the arena, he made his way to the armory, located outside the bowl-shaped arena beside the Sceyrah's Tower. Unless his plan went flawlessly, he thought to himself, he would have need of some weapons before the day was through; and if he would need some weapons, so would she.

20

The Master Swordsman waited until nightfall, and then made his way down into the catacombs. After making sure he was alone in the corridor outside the entrance to the dungeons, he quickly opened the door and stepped into the darkness. He slowly made his way down the winding staircase, glad that his Krayven's eyes could penetrate the near pitch-black gloom. In his mind he saw what his bird saw, a slowly curving set of stone stairs, unlit torches mounted to the walls at set intervals. After a few minutes he could hear the murmurs of the guards down below. He fished the package he'd prepared earlier that day out of the folds of his cloak, and as he neared the end of the stairs he struck his flint and carefully lit a small fuse that was attached to the small square box he held in his hands. Then he sent his bird ahead of him, and the Krayven flew down onto the last step and hopped around the corner, giving its master a view of the small room containing the guards.

There were two guards on duty, and they were seated at a low table, a single candle illuminating its surface. They seemed to be playing a drinking game involving cards and a bottle of strong liquor.

This may be easier than I thought, the Master considered with a small smile. The bottle was already half empty, and the guards were showing clear signs of intoxication. Just before the

fuse ran out, the Master threw the box around the corner towards the guards, and before they had a chance to figure out what was happening, the box exploded.

Such devices as this exploding box were unknown to regular soldiers, but every Master Sceyrah was trained in the secret arts of war, including the uses of powders, potions, and certain deadly magics. This particular package, a small innocuous box, contained a powder that, when exploded, released a cloudy vapor that knocked out anyone within range as soon as they inhaled it. The Master Swordsman had put enough powder in the box to create a vapor that would instantly engulf an area roughly five feet by five feet. Still, to be safe he hung back, remaining out of sight just around the corner, which was a good ten feet away from the guards. He had called his bird back to his shoulder as he had thrown the box, not wanting to knock the Krayven unconscious along with the guards. He heard their bodies hit the floor, and after waiting another thirty seconds or so for the vapor to dissipate, he entered the small guardroom.

He knew there wouldn't be a changing of the guard until morning, but he still wanted to move as quickly as possible. The small explosion had snuffed out the guard's candle, so he re-lit it using the flint in his pocket, and then he found the guard's keys hanging on a hook on the wall above the table. One of the keys opened the door leading to the cells, and he quickly stepped through the doorway, holding the candle in front of him as he did so. He began walking down the narrow hallway, knocking on each cell door as he passed by, waiting to hear a response. After trying ten doors, he heard a man's voice call out from behind the door he'd just rapped with his knuckles. The Master Swordsman unlocked the door, and found Ibn huddled in the far corner of the room, terrified.

"Please let me go!" he begged.

"Do you know which cell they put the Sceyrah in?" the Master asked Ibn, ignoring his plea.

"I think she is beside me," Ibn said, pointing to his left. Then he looked again at the Master, a quizzical expression on his face. "Who are you?" he asked. "You're not one of the guards, and you have a Krayven."

"It's not important who I am. What matters is that you and the Sceyrah will be killed at dawn unless you come with me right now."

The Master's initial plan had been to free only Lilija, but after seeing this pathetic High Priest cowering in the corner of his cell he felt pity for the small man. Going to the cell beside Ibn's, he unlocked it. The door swung open and Lilija flew at him with a shriek, but he had been expecting this. If he had been the one locked up, he would have tried to fight his way to freedom as well.

"Stop!" he shouted as he stepped back, holding up his hands, "It's me!" Lilija caught herself just as she was about to throw a punch, her fury turning to surprise at the sight of the Master Swordsman.

"What are *you* doing here? Did they send you to fetch us for punishment?"

"No. They have decided to execute both of you at dawn, but I can't let that happen. I'm here to help you escape." Despite her attempts to mentally prepare herself for the possibility that her punishment would be death, Lilija was still shocked to hear that execution had been chosen.

"Why are you helping us? When they find out, they will kill you for helping us escape."

"Don't worry about me," the Master responded quietly to Lilija, "what's important is that you escape. Quickly now, we need to move fast." From under his cloak the Master produced a sword, which he gave to Lilija. By this time Ibn had joined them in the hallway, looking frail and scared in the flickering candlelight. The Master Swordsman led them back the way he had come. The guards were still unconscious and would remain so for at least another six

hours. They made their way up the winding staircase, and when they reached the top the Master motioned for Lilija and Ibn to stop as he opened the door. Once he was convinced that no one was out walking in this part of the catacombs, he motioned for them to follow him.

He led them to another door, located just a short distance from the entrance to the dungeons. He fetched a small bottle out of a pocket in his cloak, and holding it very carefully he pulled out the cork stopper and dipped a small linen-wrapped swab inside. Even more carefully, he pulled the swab out and began wiping it on the large heavy-looking lock that hung on the door.

"This door opens into a hallway that runs under the City for quite a ways. At its end you will find a small set of stairs that lead to a set of iron bars, or so I've been told. I myself have never seen it, as I do not possess the keys necessary to open either the door or the iron bars. This liquid, however, is more than a match for any lock." Lilija watched in amazement as the lock, now soaked in this liquid, began to melt. Soon there was a pile of sizzling molten metal on the floor, and the door opened easily.

"Use this liquid to melt the lock on the iron bars, and once you have opened and passed through this iron gate you should find yourselves in a cave outside the City. Where you go from there is up to you. It's best if you don't tell me where you might go, as I'm sure to be tortured once they discover that I'm the one who helped you. I don't expect to be able to bear up indefinitely under torture, no one can." "Please don't stay, you can come with us," Lilija pleaded, dismayed at the thought of this brave man being tortured for her sake. The Master Swordsman simply shook his head and gently steered her towards the opening.

"I must stay. If I can delay their discovery of your escape, and then delay them further when they try to figure out where you've gone, then that is what I must do. I wish to give you as much of a

head-start as possible. Here, take this." He pressed a small leather purse into her hand. "It's not a lot, but there are enough silver coins in here to help both of you get a fair distance from the City, should you choose to buy a horse or hire passage on a coach. You must escape: I cannot bear the thought of your death." His voice grew quieter, and he grasped her arms firmly as he gazed down at her, saying "I have loved you for a long time, for your beauty and strength. You are dearer to me than anything."

"I know," Lilija whispered softly, "I..." but the words she wanted to say in response caught in her throat, and as tears formed in her eyes she broke free from his grip, hating herself for leaving this man she had begun to love, but knowing that she had no choice. Without looking back Lilija and Ibn hurried down the long hallway, and as Lilija heard the door close behind them she fought back the tears that threatened to overwhelm her.

21

Lilija and Ibn found the end of the corridor to be exactly as the Master Swordsman had described it. They broke through the gate using the liquid the Master had given them, and then they found themselves in a cave. Stepping outside, they had a good view of the City, which was now almost a mile away to the north. The beginnings of a plan began to form in Lilija's mind, but it was a plan that didn't involve Ibn. She turned to Ibn and asked, "Where are you going to go from here?"

Ibn thought for a moment, then answered, "I have always wanted to see the labyrinths of the Sand Scribes. I read a scroll in the Tower library that seems to hint at how to get there. If you like, you could accompany me. Perhaps you could join the Sand Warriors. They would gladly accept someone of your skill."

"Thank you, but no. I have decided to go north instead of south. Be careful in your journey, avoid people as much as possible. The City is sure to send soldiers to every town in the area." Ibn nodded in agreement, and then the two of them walked out of the cave.

After wishing each other good luck and dividing the Master's coins between them, Lilija struck out to the east, wanting to get a good distance away from the City before turning north. There was a village directly east of Tratalja, and even though it was still dark Lilija made sure to avoid the village entirely. Once past the

village, she came upon a farm. She decided to risk getting close. She needed a horse if she was going to outrun the soldiers that were sure to pursue once their escape was discovered, and the farm looked prosperous enough to have at least one horse. She crept closer, keeping as low as possible in the tall grasses. As the eastern sky began to glow, Lilija could make out the barn door. There was still no sign of movement from the stone house near the barn, so Lilija stood up and ran out of the tall grasses and onto the hard dirt-packed yard to the barn door.

She opened the door and slipped inside. There were two stalls. The first one was empty, but the second had a healthy-looking black horse. When she looked around to see if there was a saddle and other gear, she saw a flash of movement in her peripheral vision followed by a searing pain between her eyes, and after that everything went black.

When she awoke, it was bright outside, the light shining through the gaps between the slats of wood that composed the walls of the barn. The pain in her head was intense, but she had lots of experience dealing with pain, so she was able to ignore the throbbing in her skull. She tried to move, but discovered that she was tied to one of the stalls, her arms lashed tightly behind her. She was sitting with her back to the stall, her legs stretched out in front of her. Then she heard a voice.

"So you're awake, finally." The voice belonged to a dirty middle-aged man, who came into her field of vision as he spoke. "What are you doing on my farm, sneaking around? Want to steal my horse?" Lilija said nothing in reply, she simply stared up at him. Without warning he slapped her, hard, and almost instantly she tasted blood in her mouth. He leered at her, and for a moment Lilija thought he meant to strike her again, but instead he began fumbling with his pants. It was like someone had doused her with freezing cold water.

She knew what he intended to do, and the shock and horror of the knowledge chilled her to the bone.

She closed her eyes, not wanting to see him with his pants off. He grabbed her breasts, and she could smell his foul breath. He loosened the ropes that tied her to the stall, then using that slack he forced her to lay down. Then he grabbed at the rope that tied her feet together, and a spark of hope flew into Lilija's mind.

In order to rape her, he needed her legs untied. She waited until her legs were free, and as soon as he forced her legs apart she twisted her hips and kicked her right leg into his left shoulder, spinning him around. Then simultaneously she kicked her left leg up, grazing his head, while her right leg looped around his throat. Then she hooked her left foot under her right ankle and pulled up and towards herself, squeezing with all her strength. Now her two legs acted as a vice around his throat, and before he had time to react she was choking him. His face grew purple as he frantically groped and clawed at her calves, all to no avail. In mere moments, his eyes drooped, then his whole body relaxed and he fell to the dirt floor, unconscious.

Using her legs, she dragged his body as close to her hands as she could. She managed to grab the knife on his belt, and quickly sawed through the ropes that tied her hands behind her back. Soon she was free, and she stood over her would-be rapist. At first she wanted to kill him, but then a new thought presented itself. She bent down, and with a few quick strokes of the knife blade she castrated him. She quickly packed the wound with some dirty rags she found nearby, not wanting him to bleed to death. Then she cut the lobes of his ears off, a final humiliation. All slaves in Tratalja's empire had their ear lobes cut off, to mark them as property. This was a punishment much better than death, she thought. Let him live the rest of his life in impotence and shame.

She found her sword lying next to a saddle in the corner of the barn, and she quickly strapped her blade to her waist. Then she grabbed the saddle, and after throwing a blanket on the horse she strapped the saddle to its back. There was already a bit and bridle in the horse's mouth. She led the horse outside, and judging by the sunlight that confronted her and made her pounding headache even worse, it was nearly noon. She would have to be careful. Their escape from Tratalja would be well known by now, and soldiers would be roaming the countryside looking for her and Ibn. There was no sign of life from the farmhouse as she rode by. Perhaps this farmer lived by himself. She rode quickly, glad to discover that his horse seemed to be in fairly good health. It was high-spirited, a stallion, and was constantly chomping at the bit. For awhile she let it run, and they made good time. By nightfall the City was far to their south and west, and they were riding a fair ways east of the Eygil river. Lilija hoped that the soldiers would concentrate on the villages closer to the river.

It seemed that they did, or at least Lilija saw no signs of any other riders out on the grassy plains this far east. She rode as fast as she could without hurting her horse, and by the end of the week the forest was in sight. That night she made camp in the trees. The next day she began tracking the Blood-eaters. She rode west, following game trails, until she found evidence of human traffic. At first there were only the occasional tracks, but as she continued west they increased in number. She surmised that at least some of the tracks must belong to the Blood-eaters that had fled into these trees for protection after the battle. The tracks were showing signs of age, so they couldn't have stayed here long. They must have continued deeper into the forest, and sure enough, as Lilija turned north the tracks continued, and grew fresher. She was getting closer to her objective: she was going to find that young man, that boy, who had fought so well with such little skill, and she was going to finish what had been started.

CREATORS AND THE CREATED

The jailers tortured the Master Swordsman for five days before giving up.

"He doesn't know where they've gone," the Master Jailer informed Agathos. "We have broken him, and he gives us details of where they've gone, but he can't keep the details straight. The next day he contradicts himself. I think he simply wants the torture to end, so he is telling us what he thinks we want to hear in the hopes that we will be satisfied. Shall I kill him?" Agathos looked angry, but resigned. He simply nodded at the Jailer and then strode off, climbing the stairs that led out of the dungeons.

The Master Swordsman was glad to see the Jailer return with a sword, and as he waited for the blade to take off his head and end his suffering he prayed a quick prayer to the gods, asking them to help Lilija. In the forest far to the north, his prayer was answered. And then his unspoken prayer, the hidden desire within his heart, was answered as well.

The Master Swordsman's eyes opened. The confusion was nearly total. Only a moment ago he'd been waiting for death, anticipating the moment that the Jailer's sword would take off his head. Now he was looking through his eyes, eyes that should be utterly lifeless, unseeing, embedded in a bodiless head that would soon be burned along with the rest of his physical vessel. How was it that he was seeing, and seeing a place unlike any he'd ever been to??

His next thought prompted him to quickly reach up and feel his neck, and sure enough, he was completely intact. He was not in some strange disembodied state, a hallucination brought on by the nearness of death or by the few brief seconds after a death blow had been delivered when his brain might still be able to formulate thoughts and produce pictures of places too bizarre to imagine in the normal course of one's day. Where in the Hells was he?? he asked himself again. This place was foggy, white, yet with colors just beyond his vision, or so it seemed at first. There were sounds too, beautiful sounds, similar to some of the music a person could experience in the cosmopolitan city of Tratalja, but much more beautiful, harmonious. He had heard some of the traveling musicians play in the streets of Tratalja, and once a year there was the big summer festival, the celebration of abundance and harvest that was always accompanied by the most lavish spectacles the City and its wealthier citizens could afford.

Try as he might, however, he couldn't place the tune he was hearing in this strange, soft place. It was entirely foreign to his ears, and yet somehow recognizable, as though a part of him had heard it once, long ago, and was just now beginning to remember it again. As he struggled to understand what was happening to him, what he was hearing and seeing, a figure appeared. It was an old man with a gentle smile, an old man who looked strong despite his age, and who spoke as he walked closer to the Master Swordsman.

"You have died. The Jailer's sword did its work, and now you are in the land of spirits, where gods and people sometimes walk together." Things were beginning to make sense to the Master Swordsman as he listened to the old man's words. So this is what it's like to be dead. He'd grown up with the religion of the priests in the Temple complex, and he knew that the gods, in particular the four Creators who were said to have made the whole world, awaited everyone who died. Those who had lived a good life were given a chance to live again, whereas those who'd led evil lives were tortured in the many different hells that existed solely to punish the evildoer.

"Are you a god?" the Master asked the old man.

"Oh no, I am not!" the old man chuckled as he answered. "I am a man, as you are. I died a short time ago, and have been living here with the spirits. I was not given the chance to live again, but I have been given the chance to make some things right, to help those who need help, and hopefully to assist even the gods as they struggle to bring harmony back to our world. It is the gods, and only the gods, who can grant new life. And they only grant new life to the worthy."

The old man's voice had begun to lose some of its gentle humor, and the Master could tell that there was sorrow behind his words. Clearly the elderly man had died leaving things undone, and the gods would never allow such a person to receive the highest blessings of the afterlife. But apparently they didn't simply send such a person to the eternal hells either, despite what the priests always said.

"Are you here to judge me?" the Master asked. "I have lived an honorable life serving the City, but I have not been overly religious. I am sure the gods are aware that I did not give myself wholly to their worship, as many of the others did."

"Yes, they know that, and it will probably surprise you greatly to know that they don't care even a tiny bit about that. What concerns them is the life you lived. I have been told that they wish to speak with you directly. I must tell you that this is rare. Although I have only been dead a short while, I have come to learn many things in that time, and from what I've learned the gods almost never speak to the dead. That is a job left to spirits such as myself. We help the dead make the transition from one life to another, whether it's a new life in the world you just left, or whether it's a new life as a spirit, or whether it's a life of punishment in the hells below. There is one god in particular who wishes to speak with you. You will go to him now. Don't be afraid. It is a very strange sensation, or so I have been told. It will feel like your body is being pulled apart, but there is no pain. Wait until your body feels whole again, then open your eyes. You will be in the presence of the gods, or perhaps just the one, I don't know."

The Master Swordsman's heart was racing. He was going to the gods! What in the Hells could they possibly want with him? He was fairly sure he wasn't going to be punished, for he felt certain he'd led a good life, and from what this old man had said it wasn't a huge concern that he didn't worship the gods like some of the fanatics in the City. Did they have something special for him, a new life they needed him to adopt? All his thoughts and questions raced around in his mind, and then they were suddenly stilled as the place he was standing disappeared. And then he felt it. His body was separating. To say it was a strange sensation, as the old man had said, was the biggest understatement the Master had ever heard. The old man had definitely not experienced this first hand, otherwise he would have been much more expressive in his description.

The Master felt a simultaneous swirling as his body separated into smaller and smaller pieces, smaller than the tiniest snowflakes that accompanied the first storms of winter. How he felt no pain,

he had no idea. This should be excruciating, but instead it felt like nothingness, as though he was simply a rain cloud dispersing after having released all its pent up water. Faster and faster he swirled, quicker and quicker his body dissipated into who knows where, and then just as suddenly as it had begun, it ended. He opened his eyes as soon as his body felt whole again, and standing right in front of him was the most beautiful, powerful, and graceful man he had ever seen. His eyes were dark, his hair almost as black as pitch but with hints of brown. He stood at least a head taller than the Master, even though the Master Swordsman was already a tall man in comparison to his peers.

The man who stood before him exuded a fierce kind of energy unlike anything the Master had ever experienced. And then this amazing creature spoke, and the Master nearly fell to his knees in awe as the voice shook him through and through.

"My name is Huracan. It is I, along with Aiyana, who have been watching your world and working for its restoration. There were originally four, and they made everything you see. Two are still here, but the other two have passed into shadow, through the fault of one of them but not the other. Aiyana and I have seen your life, and have marveled not only at your bravery, but your extreme sacrifice made in love. You willingly gave up your life to save the one you loved even more than yourself. This sacrifice is reserved for the purest of hearts, for the person whose love and strength is virtually unparalleled in the created world. For those who exhibit such a character, the choice is given that I am giving you. You may ascend, if you so desire. Your work in the world is done, and has been done with great honor. You saved the life of one who is very important to us. Lilija, the one you love more than any other, is hoped to become part of the salvation of many peoples, a bringer of harmony and balance, a victor of good over evil.

"You can choose to remain, and be a spirit such as Hrund, who received you right after your death. Or you can be born again, and live another life that will be marked with similar bravery and honor, of that I have little doubt. Or you can ascend. To ascend is to become like me, like all of our kin, who live to create. You will become a maker of worlds, a Creator, who does the will of our Mother in all things, everywhere. Together with our kin you will travel the universe, through the stars, making life and beauty flourish everywhere you go. And you will have a name, a name of your own choosing, for you were never given a name. You were born to those who did not want you, who gave you up to the Temple and its priests. You served them well, but always you sought to serve what's best, what is always right and good, even when it went against the very priests who claim to know the good and the right. In this, you are rare. In this, you have earned the right to become one of us. What do you choose?"

The shock, as strong as it was, was beginning to wear off. It was being replaced by wonder and joy, a joy so all-encompassing that the words to describe it were unable to keep up with the Master's feelings. He simply gazed into the eyes of this man, this god, or whatever he was. Despite their fierceness, the strength that lay deep behind the eyes of this god-man were filled with a love and graciousness that the Master Swordsman had rarely seen in life. It was a kindness that went far beyond simple generosity of spirit or caring concern. Once again words failed him completely.

"I will ascend, but only if I can call you brother." The Master had made his choice, and he spoke his heart's desire. The tall man's face directly across from him broke out into a wide smile, the only answer the Master needed, and they embraced as brothers. Then he chose a name, as they continued to talk with each other, as the bonds of kinship were forged. He was no longer a simple

swordsman, a servant of a religion and a City in a world that had rejected him.

The name he chose was an ancient name, one he'd learned as a boy. The name had belonged to a hero of old, one of the great ancestors of the peoples of the north. This hero had conquered an enemy, a vast enemy who had tried to conquer the lands now being held by Tratalja. This hero, whose name had been Daimones, had led a much smaller army composed of warriors and farmers and nomadic hunters against a heathen horde from the east. Daimones had died in the great battle, but not before fighting with such ferocity and valor that he couldn't help but inspire the rag-tag army that followed him. This inspired army, composed of untrained farmers and semi-skilled warriors and hunters, managed to defeat the much larger and more powerful army of its enemy. This ancient hero, who was looked up to by every single soldier in Tratalja, and who continued to inspire armies and assassins wherever his story was told, had been named Daimones. And now it was the Master's name too.

23

THE CREATED

After three days of walking south, Ibn lucked out. A caravan of merchants, many of them pulling now-empty carts and larger wagons
behind horses and camels, overtook Ibn on the road as they were
heading back south after trading their wares in Tratalja. At first Ibn
cursed himself for sticking to the main road and allowing himself
to be seen, but as it turned out, either the merchants hadn't heard
about any escaped convicts from the City, or they simply didn't
care. One of the merchants agreed to let Ibn ride with him in his
wagon in exchange for one piece of silver, and not for the first time
since fleeing the City Ibn silently thanked the Master Swordsman.

Ibn learned from the merchant he was riding with that this
particular caravan was headed to a village on the outskirts of
the great desert, along the western coast. Ibn asked if there was
anyone in the village who would be willing to guide him through
the desert to the Sand Scribes. The merchant simply laughed. Ibn
was crestfallen, but later that week he got a bit of good news. Word
had been spreading that the small man who'd joined their caravan

was looking to go into the desert to find the Sand Scribes, and that evening Ibn was approached by another merchant.

The caravan had stopped for the night, and Ibn was eating dinner when the merchant joined him beside the campfire.

"I hear you are looking for a guide to take you to the Sand Scribes."

"Yes, I am!" Ibn replied, hope lighting up his face. "Can you take me there?"

"Yes, I can guide you, if you have money."

Ibn hesitated, then nodded, saying, "I have a little." There was a hungry look on the merchant's face that made Ibn a little uncomfortable, but he dismissed his worries, telling himself that his nerves were causing him to imagine things. After all, he was already exhausted, not being used to so much exercise. The life of a priest, or a scribe for that matter, required very little physical exertion. Most of one's time was spent in study, or in preparation and execution of weekly religious ceremonies, or in navigating through the endless and dangerous political seas. Such navigation was a crucial skill: Ibn learned early that there were many hidden reefs and barely submerged rocks in the political waters that constituted Tratalja's priestly class, and not knowing about such dangers could result in a very brief career as a priest. The most dangerous rock that could destroy a priest's career was Agathos. Ibn decided that it would take awhile for his body to get used to all this physical activity, and to stop sensing danger when there was none.

It took two and a half more weeks before they reached the village. During that time Ibn could have sworn that the days were getting longer and hotter. He was always sweating, and the only relief came at night when the barren land cooled off. There were occasional clusters of trees, but for the most part the landscape was flat and empty, or so it seemed to a City dweller like Ibn. Some of the men in the caravan would ride away for a few hours, sometimes

as long as a day, and sometimes they returned with freshly killed game. So the land couldn't be completely empty, Ibn thought. Animals lived here, and that meant there was enough grass and other plants to sustain them. At night it was not uncommon to hear the howls of coyotes, and the rare hooting of an owl, although that only happened when they were near one of those groups of trees.

Once they reached the ocean-side village, the caravan split up. It seemed that everyone in the caravan either lived or worked in and around this village. Ibn admired the exotic plant life that was in evidence all around this oasis-like village. They had left the tall grasses of the plains three weeks ago, and now the parched, hard-packed sandy ground gave way to flowering cacti and lush palm trees. The village benefited greatly from its proximity to the ocean and the regular rainfall that occurred along the coastline. Ibn's heart had soared at the sight of a populated place. It was an oasis from more than just barren flat-lands, it was also a much needed break from the stark loneliness of riding through a region utterly devoid of human presence beyond those with whom he rode.

Ibn openly gawked at this small town, taking in the beautiful palm trees that gently swayed in the ocean breeze, the fern shrubs and tall wide grasses that grew closer to the beach. The flowers, not just from cacti but from other trees and bushes, gave the town an almost garden-like feel, similar to the brief glimpse inside the King's palace that Ibn had experienced five years previous. But everything in the King's palace had been brought from somewhere else. Here, such beauty grew naturally, and that seemed to make it even more beautiful. For Ibn, there was too much in Tratalja that seemed false, too much grandeur and wealth that was used to portray a beauty without context. Such beauty was being hijacked, its own natural power circumvented by those whose power was the real object of attention.

After making sure that he knew where to find his guide, Ibn found the only local inn and booked himself a room. After traveling for nearly four weeks Ibn felt like relaxing for a few days before braving the desert. His guide seemed anxious to get going, but Ibn convinced him to wait.

Two days later Ibn began to get restless. He'd bought everything he figured he would need for a trek into the desert: water skins, food, and light comfortable clothing made from white linen that would be cooler than the heavier garments he was currently wearing. On his third day in the village he got up early and met his guide, who was standing next to a donkey laden with supplies. His guide, who said his name was Abo, took the lead.

After only a few hours, Ibn was sweating profusely, and it was still early morning. By the time the sun had reached its zenith Ibn's forehead was dripping sweat and it felt like nearly every square inch of his clothing was soaking wet. They were almost out of sight of the village of flowers, and already Ibn missed its beauty and the cool rest the town had offered.

Abo was a silent companion, which suited Ibn well. It was too hot to talk anyway. After the second day Ibn was beginning to wonder why they didn't travel at night, when it was cooler. They could use Abo's tent as a lean-to to provide shade during the day.

Ibn never got a chance to suggest it.

That evening as they were setting up camp, Abo took advantage of Ibn's distractedness, sneaking up behind him and knocking him out with one of his heavy cooking pots. He quickly began rifling through Ibn's things, dumping out his pack and sorting through the few belongings that the priest had carried with him. Abo stopped and craned his neck. He was sure he'd heard something, a far-off screeching, but whatever it was he no longer heard it. He went back to his pillaging, not noticing the slight change in air currents caused by the folding of great wings that he never got the chance to

see. Then another horrible screech filled the air, deafeningly loud this time, not like the first faint sound Abo had thought he'd heard. He screamed in pain and shock as sharp talons punctured his shoulders and neck. His feet left the ground as the massive Raptor lifted him into the air.

Abo continued screaming as the ground rapidly disappeared beneath his feet, the darkness of early evening obscuring his view. Once the Raptor had reached a certain height, it let go, and after a few moments Abo's screams ended abruptly with a loud thud in the desert sand.

Ibn's consciousness returned slowly, and for awhile he had no clue where he was or what he was seeing. Then his foggy eyesight began to grow clearer, and as he slowly regained an awareness of his surroundings he could have sworn that he saw an old man talking with a monstrous bird. They were on the other side of the dying campfire from Ibn, and their voices were too quiet to be heard clearly. Then the old man began to fade, disappearing altogether after a few more seconds under Ibn's squinty, pain-filled gaze.

Ibn struggled to his feet, his fear compelling him to ignore the throbbing in his head. He wanted to get away from this bird, this massive creature who may very well wish to eat a small man such as himself. As he tried to slink into the shadows, however, the bird sprang upwards, and with a flap of its massive wings the bird flew straight into Ibn, knocking him onto his back. Ibn screamed as the Raptor grabbed Ibn with its talons and tossed him into the air. Before he had a chance to figure out what was happening, he was landing on the bird's back just as the bird once again sprang into the air. Clutching at the bird's neck, Ibn held on for dear life as they rocketed into the air.

The cold night air whipped all around Ibn as they flew higher and higher, and Ibn couldn't help but shiver. Now he wished that he was wearing his old clothes. On and on they flew, at speeds which

nearly took Ibn's breath away. As daylight began to break on the eastern horizon, the Raptor began to descend. Soon they were back on the ground, and Ibn released his death grip and began rubbing his freezing hands together. Looking around, he realized they were at the mouth of a gorge, in the middle of the sandy desert. There were high rock walls on either side of the gorge, and Ibn began thinking to himself that he knew this place. Then he remembered: he had read about it in the scroll he'd been reading before he'd been summoned to the Lord's Council. He was close to the entrance to one of the famous labyrinths of the Sand Scribes!

The bird nudged him forward, and Ibn began walking the length of the gorge. As he walked, Sand Warriors cautiously climbed down from their hidden perches, fear clearly written on their faces as they looked at the massive bird that remained crouched at the entrance to the gorge. They didn't stop Ibn, however, they simply joined him in the dusty valley, walking with him towards the hidden entrance. Perhaps they thought that any person who had flown here on a Raptor was not someone they should confront, but rather someone they should follow. Ibn didn't give it another thought. When he reached the end of the gorge, he found a large boulder resting against the base of a wide crag. He continued ignoring the Warriors who had walked with him, choosing to simply stare straight ahead, never wavering from his goal of finding and gaining entrance to one of the wonders of the ancient world.

Walking around the boulder, he found a small gap on its left side. Ibn walked through the gap and began walking along a smooth narrow tunnel that slowly opened up into a high wide hallway, with doorways on either side. These doorways opened into rooms filled with scrolls, books, and other treasures. A huge smile lit up his face as Ibn realized that after nearly a lifetime of dreaming about visiting such a place, here he was. A few startled faces poked out

from one of the rooms, and with a smile still tugging at the corners of his mouth, Ibn strode forward to introduce himself.

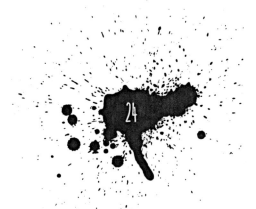

24

Lilija was riding slowly, not wanting to miss any tracks that would suggest where the Blood-eaters were going, when she thought she heard a voice. She reigned in her horse, her body tense. She heard it again, or rather she thought she did. Now she wasn't sure. The voice was more like a whispered thought, as though her mind was now entertaining someone else's mind, someone else's thoughts. It reminded her of the Oracle. The voice grew clearer.

Follow further west, then north.

The thought was clear, and for some unknown reason Lilija felt a strong urging to obey its direction. She turned her horse westward, weaving her way through the trees. Soon she found another trail, this one headed west, so she followed it. After an hour or so the voice returned, instructing her to turn north. After another few hours she spotted tracks: there were human tracks intermingled with giant paw prints. The paw prints scared her. She remembered the massive cat that had killed so many during the battle, and she was sure that these prints belonged to that same animal. She hesitated, not wanting to encounter this beast, but the voice returned, urging her forward. She gently kicked the horse's flank, and they resumed their northward course. That evening, as the sun was setting, she found them. They were encamped by a slow-moving river, nestled in a small valley. The valley itself was not as heavily

treed as the surrounding forest, allowing for good-sized clearings that could house many of the conical tents that the Blood-eaters used as dwellings.

At this point Lilija began questioning herself. Should she just ride right into their camp and announce herself? Was she insane?? These were Blood-eaters: they were known for their love of violence, a war-mongering tribal peoples if ever there was one. But then again, that could actually work in her favor, if she could convince them from the start that she too was a warrior, and a warrior who wanted the exact same thing that they did. It would take some quick acting, to ensure that they didn't simply shoot her off her horse with an arrow, or chop her head off as soon as she was close enough to one of their swords. She decided to wait and scout around their camp, hoping to find the young man she'd fought with. She had seen in his eyes the blood lust that she also felt, especially when sparring with an equal.

The lust had settled on her during the battle in almost the same measure that the young Blood-eater had shown, and despite the macabre nature of this particular pleasure, she'd discovered the thrill of taking someone's life before they can take yours. It was almost a necessary thrill, a necessary pleasure, because without it one could easily be consumed by the pure terror of war. Cowardice was the most reasonable response in the face of imminent death, but for those who were able to push past the all-too natural fear of death, the love of battle provided a welcome substitute. The visceral thrill, the indescribable joy of killing your opponent whilst death nipped at her heels, was a feeling that both scared and enticed Lilija.

The next day, after a fitful sleep some five hundred yards away from the Blood-eaters camp, Lilija rode slowly into their midst, seeing the conical tents rise out of the middle of the stand of trees that surrounded the clearing they'd chosen. She had chosen to ride

into the camp from its western side, the general area that Ari had been in yesterday as she had spied on them from a small cluster of bushes at the far western edge of the clearing. Her vantage point had been downwind at the time, so neither the Blood-eaters' horses nor their dogs had had much chance to discover her and sound the alarm. As she continued slowly riding towards the tents, the barking of dogs announced her presence. Warriors ran out to meet her, brandishing swords, and she quickly held up her hands, trying to show that she meant them no harm. Then she saw his gaunt scarred face, belonging to the boy who was more than a boy. With him stood a massive white cat.

"You!" she shouted. "It's me, we fought on the battlefield!" Ari looked surprised, and then recognition dawned on his face. He yelled something to the warriors who were advancing on Lilija, and they stopped. He began to run towards her, and Lilija swung down from her horse.

"What are you doing here? What do you want with us?" Ari asked, his face a contorted mask of scars, making it difficult to tell what, if anything, he was feeling or thinking.

"The City tried to execute me, blaming me and one other for allowing the City to be sacked. I managed to escape, and decided that I wanted to find you. I hate the City, especially the priests, for trying to kill me, for blaming me. They killed my bird, by now they've killed someone I loved, and I want revenge. You and your tribes started a war with them, and I want to help finish it. Will you let me join you, and will you help me finish what has been started? Will you help me wage war against Tratalja?"

As Ari had listened to her his scarred face began to change, and despite the difficulty in seeing past the many wounds on his face, Lilija thought she could begin to detect certain emotions: a startled surprise as she had told him what she wanted, and now a strange sort of curiosity, an almost lustful desire, seemed to be written on

the scarred canvas. Scars and lust made for a scary image, a face that made Ari seem less like a boy and more like a savage animal. Lilija waited for him to respond to what she'd said, and after a moment he did so.

"My cat has spoken to me. She tells me that she led you here, speaking to your thoughts with her thoughts. She says that the gods brought you to us, that they want us to join together, to fight together." Ari paused, then continued. "I will fight with you. Grasp my arm, and together we will destroy this City."

Vala began to growl, and with her thoughts she warned Ari, sensing what he was feeling. Ari stood there, his arm outstretched, and for a moment Lilija hesitated. The cat continued growling, and it almost looked as though a thought was passing between this beast and the scarred warrior who stood beside her. After a moment, Lilija dropped her horse's reins and strode forward. She had gambled on a good reception, and so far these savages had not killed her or even threatened to do so after Ari had stopped them. This is what she wanted. She wanted to join forces with this unskilled yet strangely mighty young man, she wanted her revenge, and she wanted to be a part of hopefully setting things right against an empire that was bent on domination.

Ari continued to hold out his good right arm, and Lilija reached forward with hers. As she reached out her right arm to take his, Ari's left arm swung around, its awkward wounded movement catching Lilija by surprise. Tightly gripped in the claw-like fingers of his scarred, fused limb, Ari held a short dagger. It plunged into Lilija's right side, sliding neatly between ribs and puncturing lung, before being pulled out as quickly as it had entered.

With a cold kind of fury fueled by his lust for blood and his hatred of the Sceyrah, Ari stabbed her again and again. The shock on Lilija's face seemed frozen in time: she hardly recognized the pain for what it was, still trying to figure out why this was

happening, what exactly was being done to her. Slowly her legs crumpled beneath her, and she sank to her knees, coming to rest in a pool of her own blood, darkened by the dirt it was mixing with. Blood-drenched stalks of grass poked through the pool, and in her shock and disorientation Lilija focused on these green sentinels, seeing their stark beauty, marveling at how they could exist so serenely in the midst of such violence. She could feel the tickle of the blades of grass between her fingers as she knelt forward, her hands splayed in front of her in a vain attempt to remain upright.

Just before she fell on her face, her head was yanked up by her hair, and she felt lips brush her ears, then heard Ari whisper, "I will drink your blood, then I will drink the blood of every last Sceyrah in Tratalja. And you will all be re-united in the lowest Hells, to burn forever."

Then Lilija remembered no more.

* * *

She awoke hundreds of miles away, standing on a green mound of earth, surrounded by tall grassy plants that reached past her thighs. There was a slight wind, and the grasses lightly brushed against her legs. An old man stood before her on the same mound. He had seemed to materialize right in front of her as she watched, taking solid form from within a light fog that hovered just above the mound. At first he reminded Lilija of the ghostly visions and nightmares she used to have as a child, and yet with him she felt no fear; instead, she was convinced, without knowing how, that he was a kind man, a good man.

She became aware that there were many grassy mounds in this clearing. They were obviously not natural formations, and then she knew that they were burial mounds. As if recalling memories from the distant past, from someone who had lived many lifetimes before her, Lilija remembered the priests talking about the burial

practices of the northern tribes and clans. The City burned their dead, believing that the soul is best sent to the afterlife in the form of smoke. The priests derided the practice of burial, preaching that such a death was never resolved. The dead remained stuck between worlds, failing to exist fully either in the world of the living or the dead.

"You are dying, Lilija," the kind old man spoke, a smile lighting his face. *Dying?* she thought. *Then why is he smiling? Is he happy I'm dying, or is he just a senile old ghost?*

"Where am I?" she asked.

"You are standing on the burial mound of my great-great-grandfather. I have brought you to this place by your spirit, for your body is greatly damaged and will soon be dead. Sometimes we can take a person, body and spirit, to a place of power such as this one. But we couldn't do so with you." Lilija touched her side, where the knife had made its mark over and over. Sure enough, there were no wounds, nothing to indicate that she had just been savagely attacked.

"What's going to happen to me now? Will I become a spirit, like you?"

"That depends," the old man replied. "Do you wish to become like me, or would you rather stay in the world you know? Before you answer, there are certain things you should know. Should you choose to live in the world you know, not even I can tell you what that will look like. The hidden gods will decide how to bring you back, and since your body is severely damaged, perhaps even dead, you may not be able to live as you were. The gods may choose to give you a rebirth, or allow you to take up the body of someone who is dying but whose body remains largely whole and undamaged. I have access to certain spirits, but not the gods who possess the power to animate life. Be careful how you choose."

Lilija thought for a long time, or at least it felt long. Time seemed irrelevant here, in this cool, still clearing. She felt light, as though at any moment she might start floating above the mound, joining the clouds in their lazy circuit around the sky. It seemed an effort to determine exactly what she was feeling. Did she want to live, to remain in this world? Or did she want to explore this strange new existence, seeing the world for what it really was, populated by the living and the dead, by gods and spirits and flesh and bone? She felt pulled in two different directions, until she thought about Ari and Tratalja. She didn't hate the Blood-eater who had viciously taken her life. He was consumed by hate, by his desire for revenge.

For Lilija, her desire was to fight, to destroy the evil that Tratalja had become. There was a certain amount of vengeance that fueled her desire, to be sure, but she also felt a righteousness, a sense that there was a great injustice that needed to be addressed. And she had the ability to fight for and gain a greater justice than Tratalja's empire had ever known. She wasn't sure exactly what her abilities were, beyond her strength and skill in combat, but she knew for certain that she possessed something no one else did, and the world needed what she had.

"I choose to stay, to live," Lilija spoke, feeling a sense of peace as she said the words aloud, feeling a confirmation within her that this was the right choice. The old man's smile, which had always lingered on his face, grew wide, and then everything melted into a strange swirling, and Lilija thought she could hear the pealing of bells, similar to the Temple bells, but more beautiful, more powerful. The sounds grew louder, the melody itself becoming more urgent, and the swirling took on a fantastic blend of colors, seeming to match the melody and tempo of the music. Then there was nothing, just a growing awareness within the blanket of darkness that surrounded her that life was beginning again, flowing again, in and around her. Finally her eyes were able to open.

Strange faces were looking down at her, faces marked by grief, many of them with fresh tears still flowing. Their looks of grief turned to shock, then they all seemed to start shouting at once. One voice rose above the others.

"She's alive!! Look, her eyes are open! She's breathing!!" The voice belonged to an older man, and before he'd finished speaking a woman had rushed closer and was cupping Lilija's face in her hands.

"The gods be praised!! Tatiana, you have returned to us!" the woman cried with joyous relief, lifting Lilija's body to her own in a crushing hug. The others that had crowded around the bed were now voicing similar prayers of thanksgiving, and Lilija began taking in more of the scene. She was in a bedroom, in what looked to be a wealthy person's home. There were frescoes painted on the walls, depicting scenes of nature. They were beautifully done, with vibrant colors and elaborate figures. Most were of animals, but some showed human figures as well. There was a forest scene with deer and a few smaller animals. Perhaps the most stunning was on the ceiling directly above her: a blue sky with white clouds, and a lone eagle soaring gracefully against the blue backdrop. More voices called the name Tatiana, and then, to Lilija's shock, a priest she recognized from her days in Tratalja approached the bed. His face was as shocked as the other mourners in the room, and he silently mouthed a prayer as he stood over her.

"It is a miracle, a genuine miracle. She had stopped breathing for more than five minutes, her heart had stopped as well. I will call for the Medicians, they will want to examine her." After saying this the priest quickly left the room, and the woman who had hugged Lilija so fiercely was still grasping her hand and lovingly stroking her face. Then Lilija spoke.

"Who is Tatiana?"

EPILOGUE

He found the perfect place. It was deep underground, a natural fissure in the rocky outcropping that permitted Kallos to go deep underground. The surrounding plains were barren except for the grasses that attracted the herds of deer and other grazing creatures, and only occasionally would people set up hunting camps anywhere near this particular cluster of rocks. In the future, that would be an entirely different story. But for now, this abnormal geological feature sitting in the middle of grassy plains seemed to Kallos the perfect spot to stash the only possession he could claim. The rock he'd made, filled with Eluthuria's blood, was now buried far away from prying eyes. The rock was cursed, he knew that only too well. The deed he'd done, Eluthuria's murder, clung to the rock by virtue of the tainted fluid it contained. If only he could take the rock down to the ocean and wash it clean, wash away the stain of his awful deed. He could see where he would go, the path he would take down to the sea. In the distance the great river emptied itself into the wide expanse of salt water, and this emptying process was beginning to forge a wider and wider bay out of solid rock. Kallos could see it from here, and he longed to wade out into the salty sea and wash the curse right out of the rock. It was foolish, he knew, utterly foolish: the urge to wash the rock was merely the desperate

173

scheming cry of a self-pitying fool. Such a curse never left, never went away.

The blood was cursed, gained as it was through treachery and violence and greed, and Kallos still hoped despite all reason that one day this small stolen treasure would be his salvation. One day, if it could ever be possible to find the means to do it, Kallos would come back to this place and unearth the only physical object his shadowy form could hold. One day he would use this blood to gain back his form. One day he would no longer be shadow, if only he could find a way. He'd already been stuck here in this awful world for nearly a million years, and everywhere he looked he was tortured by visions of his kin and the ever present reminder of his own evil.

Ugappe and Karris were everywhere, in everything and everyone. And Kallos was too, his shadow blanketing the world and its inhabitants with a kind of greyish film that only he and his former kin could see. Only those with eyes such as theirs could see the strange mixture of Creator likeness and evil shadow. Kallos was sure that the peoples of this world could feel him, of that there could be no doubt, but they didn't have eyes to see what he could see. The only thing they seemed aware of was their own reality, the wild emotions that could start a fire deep within their fragile spirits, emotions that could lead to great acts of love, and equally great acts of hate. He'd watched these humans, these glorified apes, as they'd discovered their natures and begun to act out of their own particular longings. He'd seen their capacity for love, for grace, for goodness, everything that Ugappe and Karris had imparted to them. But he'd also seen their shadows, their cravings, their sick desires for enslavement as they tried to force their individual wills on each other like dogs in a pack. Kallos hated them, hated all of them, for their unceasing reminders of his own dark failing. And so Kallos waited, hoping

against every possible hope that one day a path would appear, a way would open up, and Kallos would set himself free.

Acknowledgements

The author would like to thank the following people for their invaluable feedback: Dr. Timothy Harvie, Colleen Derksen, Norm Quantz, and the author's wonderful wife Michelle.

The genesis of this storyline can be attributed to one person, my mentor Norman Quantz, who encouraged me to re-awaken my love of writing fiction after I told him that I'd written a novel while in Junior High School. When he learned this about me, he asked me why I was working construction instead of writing. This simple question lit a spark in me, and that night when I went home I began sketching out the background information that eventually became the landscape occupied by Tratalja and the Blood-eaters.

For those who are interested, my copy editor, Colleen Derksen, has an excellent blog on parenting and spirituality. Check it out: http://displaythesplendorofgod.blogspot.ca/

Finally, please check out my blog "Books and Chatter" http://framingtimothy.blogspot.ca/ and while there I strongly encourage you to click on the link to learn more about my mentor, Norm Quantz. He is an invaluable resource if you're interested in life-long learning and being mentored in order to achieve your maximum potential.

CPSIA information can be obtained at www.ICGtesting.com
Printed in the USA
LVOW080351190313

324836LV00001B/11/P